WINGS OF LOVE

A Lilac Novel
By
Pamela Ferguson

Dedication

To romance writers Letty James and Alyssa Roberts, for offering constructive feedback when I needed it most. Without your friendship and encouragement this book would not have been written.

Chapter One

Too late to turn back now.

Sweat streamed down Jack's face as he jogged past dilapidated vehicles and boarded-up storefronts. The early May sun, unseasonably hot, beat down on his shoulders, burning the back of his neck. If it weren't for the gang-symbol graffiti and distant Washington, D.C. skyline, he could almost imagine himself back in a war zone.

Marco's men were posted along rooftops and slouching in doorways. Their hawk-like gazes had tracked him for three blocks, assessing the threat he posed. Maybe he should've brought another Peacetalker. But Marco's invitation had been explicit. Come alone.

He stopped in front of a ramshackle house and lifted the lower edge of his tee shirt to wipe the sweat from his face. See guys, no wire. No weapons.

"Come on," a male voice ordered from the dark interior.

He followed Marco's man through the dimly lit hall. The guy had missed his calling. With a build like that he could've easily been a professional linebacker. Or a Green Beret.

Thick curtains covered the windows. A group of young men sat crowded around a large flat screen television, engrossed in a first-person shooter game. Electronic explosions mingled with curses and verbal jibes as the players battled for dominance. Ash trays overflowed with cigarette butts. Empty pizza boxes and drink cans littered the floor. The scene wasn't all that different from a frat house.

Except these guys were criminals.

Marco sat in the corner, hunched over his laptop. The gang leader had the piercing eyes of a leopard, the quick movements of a feral cat who could dominate one second and disappear the next. A man like Marco never met anyone in the same place twice.

"Jackie, my man. Thank you for accepting my invitation. Sit down." The black-inked skulls and scrolls on Marco's tattoo-covered arms told the story of gang affiliations and repeat jail time. "Where you been keeping yourself?"

Jack straddled the chair, resting his forearms on the back. "Wherever Steve sends me."

"You need a new boss. I can always use a man who knows his way around an AK-47."

He'd told Marco about his past experience as an army negotiator the first time they'd been introduced. Building the fragile trust that existed between criminals and mediators meant sharing information. For Peacetalkers, there could be no hidden agenda, no personal stake in the outcome of any negotiation. The only goal was peace.

Marco leaned back and spread his arms. "So, who's making deliveries at the soup kitchen in my territory? Peacetalkers and I had a deal it was off limits."

Jack trained his gaze on Marco's face. If the gang leader lied, he'd see the evidence in his eyes. "I hear it's one of your men."

"No way. Anybody doing deals at Father Jim's?" Marco called to the young men seated around the TV.

At the sound of Marco's voice, gaming and shouting stopped. All heads whipped around. A dozen sets of eyes trained on their leader like a pack of hounds transfixed by the hunter's command. Each man shook his head in silent response.

Marco spread his hands. "See. Not my guys."

The men resumed playing.

"Diners are complaining," Jack continued, his tone intentionally flat. "The police wanted to post an officer during meal times but Father Jim refused. Won't even let them install a surveillance camera."

Marco smiled, flashing his gold grills. "Father Jim's got cred."

Jack nodded. The elderly priest insisted his soup kitchen served all God's children, not just the law-abiding ones. "Sounds like the Peacetalkers have more work to do."

"Then do it," Marco said, his tone dismissive as he looked down at his laptop.

Meeting adjourned. Not a head turned as Jack walked out.

Marco's bodyguard led Jack to the sidewalk. "Not everybody's here," the man muttered, his lips barely moving.

Jack stared into the distance, keeping his expression neutral. Message received.

"Later, man." He took off jogging, arriving twenty minutes later at the Metro parking garage where he'd left his pickup. His heart pounded as his truck crawled through city traffic. He'd clean up and head into the office. He needed to tell Steve the rumor they'd heard might be true. One of Marco's men could be selling drugs in the soup kitchen behind the gang leader's back.

Slipping into an empty parking slot, he raced into his apartment building and up the steps. Half way down the hallway he reached for his keys and froze. The hairs on the back of his neck stood up. He looked over his shoulder.

A young man dressed in black stepped out of the shadow. "You're looking for who's selling at the soup kitchen." The dim light revealed the sheen of sweat on his brow, the fire of anger in his dark eyes.

"Marco was already looking before he called me." Jack spoke in the steady monotone he'd been trained to use in tense situations. "Father Jim's is a drug-free zone. Everybody knows that."

Light flickered on the blade the young man held in his shaking hand. "Marco declared war on whoever's dealing there."

Jack wished suddenly for the gun he'd given up when he'd chosen to become a Peacetalker. "Let's go to the police together. You'll get a lighter sentence if—"

"You think Marco can't reach into jail and punish me?" the young man snapped. The knife flashed.

Jack leapt to the side. The men tumbled to the floor, kicking the walls as they struggled. He winced as the knife sliced through his shirt.

An apartment door opened and somebody yelled. His attacker jumped to his feet and ran. Head throbbing, Jack listened to a distant voice calling the police. He heard the sound of fluttering wings just before everything went black.

~

Reo Greene inhaled the fresh mountain breeze, the scent of lilacs tickling her nose. Main Street pulsed with the sound of pounding feet. She took a cup of water from the table in front of the library and offered it to a woman running past. "Great job! Way to go!"

She glanced down the street at the town hall clock. Not much longer and the race would be over. She took a deep breath and rolled her head from side to side, wincing at the tension in her neck. She'd put off her teaching methods research paper longer than she should have. But when she'd signed up to coordinate Lilac's first 5K race, she hadn't realized it was being held the weekend before final exams. Once she completed all the work for her online college classes, she could focus on practicing for her job interview. Everyone said she was a shoo-in for a teaching job at Lilac Mountain High School.

She looked around and smiled. She'd never seen Main Street so alive on a Saturday morning. The sleepy Virginia mountain town had been preparing for this day for months. Brick-front shop windows contained brightly colored displays. Spectators lined the sidewalks, cheering on friends and family members as they jogged past. She pulled out her phone and took some pictures for the town's social media page. She turned around to take a selfie with the finish line behind her.

Welcome Home, Jack Warfield!

The white welcome banner strung above Main Street billowed into her camera's view. She scowled. She'd heard Jack Warfield was coming back. Had won a medal and gotten out of the army.

With any luck, she wouldn't have to see him.

She lowered her phone and looked directly into the sympathetic gaze of Miss Emma, the town librarian.

The older woman stood at the next water table, filling cups. "You're not worried about seeing Jack again, are you?"

My, oh my, Miss Emma didn't miss a trick. And she didn't think twice about saying exactly what was on her mind. Reo sniffed. "He should be worried about seeing me."

Miss Emma tilted her head. "Over five years have passed. Hope you two can let bygones be bygones."

Reo reached for an empty cup and filled it. "I won't start anything if he doesn't."

Miss Emma nodded her approval, then waved at a group of teenage runners. "Over four hundred participants. Can you believe it? Who said nobody would show up?"

Reo glanced around, studying the crowd. "It's hard to tell if there are more townies or more newcomers." Since the solar plant had opened a few years back, Lilac's modest population had almost doubled. Townies made a point of complaining about the crowds whenever they couldn't find a Main Street parking space or had to wait in line too long at Allen and Eva's Organic Produce.

Miss Emma continued to hand water to passing runners. "They're doing an activity together, that's the important thing. And the town has you to thank for coordinating it. That will look great on your resume." She nudged Reo's arm as Principal Owens and some of the high school teachers ran by and waved.

"I only organized it," Reo protested, waving back to her—fingers crossed—future boss and coworkers. "The race was your idea."

"You probably shouldn't say that too loudly." Miss Emma inclined her head towards Mayor Tom Burgin who stood at the finish line, high-fiving the runners. She frowned. "Bad enough the mayor pooh-poohed the race when I suggested it. Then he turned around and made it sound like his own idea at the next town council meeting. I tell you, my jaw hurt for a week from the tongue lashing I gave him." She patted Reo's hand. "But he made up for it by putting you in charge. The town can always trust you to do things right."

Reo bit her tongue. When she'd agreed to organize the race, she'd had no idea how much time it would take. With all the squabbling over how the event would impact Main Street businesses and other Saturday morning activities, you'd think she was coordinating an Olympic marathon. She picked up her clipboard and studied her checklist. She hadn't forgotten anything. If things continued to go smoothly, she'd be back working on her research paper before lunch.

Miss Emma's short silver curls bobbed in the breeze as she walked over to Reo's table. "Even before I told off Mayor Burgin at the town council meeting, he wasn't talking to me. We haven't had a pleasant conversation in years."

"How come?"

Miss Emma leaned against Reo's shoulder. "Honey,

I'd tell you if I could remember." She burst out laughing.

"You ladies gonna let me in on the joke?" Lavinia Burgin tottered towards their table, diamond pendant glistening at the neckline of her bright pink jogging outfit. Wearing a matching diamond tennis bracelet and two massive diamond stud earrings, the mayor's wife was a walking advertisement for her jewelry shop, Sparkles Galore.

Miss Emma cleared her throat. "That sun is fierce. The mayor must be feeling hotter than a sun-scorched gecko. Think he might like a drink?"

Lavinia whirled around. "Oh, my goodness, his face is beet red. I told him to wear a hat!" She glanced at the steady stream of runners then down at her platform sandals. "Reo, honey, you're wearing sensible shoes. Be a darling and run a drink out to him."

Miss Emma extended a cup to Lavinia, eyebrows lifted. "Don't you think the mayor would prefer receiving a drink from his wife? Reo is not your go-fer."

Lavinia scowled. "Honestly, Emma, I'm wearing four-inch heels. I'm just asking Reo to do me a favor."

Miss Emma held the cup steady. Lavinia refused to take it.

Reo pushed a stray lock out of her eyes and tucked it into her pony tail. Really? Miss Emma and Lavinia were going to start something now? It had been awkward enough growing up in a town where every adult female behaved as if she had a say in how Reo should be raised. She shot Miss Emma a please-don't-do-this look, took the cup, and smiled at Lavinia. "No problem. I'll take it to him."

She waited at the curb near the finish line, looking for a break in the runners. After a cluster of teenagers passed, she stepped into the street. "Here you go, Mayor—Oomph!"

The cup sailed out of her hand, splashing water into her eyes. Legs tangled with hers as her elbow connected with something hard. She heard a grunt as a pair of strong hands wrapped around her waist, steadying her while runners hurried past. The scent of orange juice and spicy, masculine soap washed over her. She blinked hard to clear her vision.

"You okay?" a male voice asked.

Jack Warfield's chiseled face hovered inches above hers. His dark-eyed gaze studied her, surprised. Hints of the rebel who'd left five years ago lingered at the edges of his wary expression. Muscled arms held her close like they had only one time before.

She gulped, her face warm, and squirmed out of his grasp. "I'm fine."

Sunlight glinted off the chestnut hair tumbling over his forehead. The corner of his mouth curled. "Wish I could say the same for the mayor."

She whirled around. Mayor Burgin had moved to the sidewalk. Lavinia stood beside him, pressing a paper towel to his cheek. The front of his red polo shirt was splattered with water.

"Oh, no." Reo wiped water from her cheeks as she dodged runners. "Mayor Burgin, I'm so sorry."

"It was my fault, sir." Jack joined them and extended his hand.

Her jaw dropped. Jack accepting the blame for something? That was new.

Mayor Burgin waved away the paper towel. "It'll

dry, Lavinia. A little water never hurt anybody. You two okay?"

She'd just collided with the one guy who hated her guts so, no, not really. She nodded, silently commanding her heart to stop pounding.

Mayor Burgin gave Jack an appraising look then clasped his hand. "Welcome home, son. Couldn't believe my ears when your uncle Pete said you were coming back for a visit." He turned to Reo. "Where are we on the schedule?"

She whirled around in a sudden panic. "Where's my clipboard?"

Jack extended his hand. "You dropped this."

Fighting the urge to grab it from him, she accepted it with a tight smile. "Thank you." She flipped through the pages while her heart galloped. Everything had been going so smoothly before Jack showed up.

She cleared her throat. "So far, so good. Filmore Hardware wants the sidewalk cleared by nine-thirty so they can put out their mowers and wheelbarrows. The flower shop can't display all their carts until we break down the stage. St. Andrew's has a wedding at eleven and needs parking space for the limo. As long as the runners finish by nine-fifteen, we should be fine."

Mayor Burgin glanced at the race clock. "Perfect. Jack, when I go on stage to announce the winners, I'd like to introduce you to the crowd, officially welcome you back, and tell the story of how you got your medal. How does that sound?"

"Thanks for the offer," Jack replied, his expression polite, "but I'd rather not."

"What?" Lavinia squawked, dropping the roll of paper towels.

Reo choked back a startled laugh. Jack shot her a sideways glance before retrieving the paper towel roll from the sidewalk and offering it to the mayor's wife. Lavinia snatched it from his grasp with a huff.

The mayor nodded, his expression serious. "Understood. Served two tours overseas myself." He waved a thumb at the welcome home banner. "How about that thing?"

Reo waited as Jack studied the banner, his expression unreadable.

"The banner was a real surprise," he said finally.

Lavinia squeezed the mayor's arm and squealed, "See, I told you he'd like it."

Mayor Burgin patted his wife's hand. His thoughtful gaze moved to Reo's face then back to Jack's. "I have a project I'd like to discuss with you two. Come by my office on Monday. Say around eleven?"

A project? She'd just finished organizing a 5K race. Reo pulled out her phone and checked her calendar. Her research paper was due by nine Monday morning. She didn't have to be at her part-time job at the DMV until after lunch. "Works for me."

Jack cleared his throat. "If you don't mind my asking, sir, what's this about?"

"Rather not discuss it here. We'll chat Monday." Mayor Burgin winked. "Almost time to announce the winners. Reo, please meet Lavinia and me at the stage area with the results."

"Okay." She waited until they left and turned to Jack. "Still stirring up trouble, I see."

"What? Saying no to the mayor or running into you?" He lifted the edge of his tee shirt to wipe the perspiration from his face.

"Did you run into me on purpose?" she challenged, refusing to let his muscled abs distract her.

He lowered his shirt and cocked his head. "You think I ran into you on purpose?"

She raised her chin. She'd be darned if he would push her around this time. "Did you?"

"Jack!" Miss Emma waved from her spot behind the water table. "Come over here so I can get a good look at you."

Reo crossed her arms, waiting.

His gaze moved from the top of her head to the toes of her running shoes and back up. "I did not run into you on purpose," he said finally. "But keep up the attitude and you'll make me wish I had." He strode across the sidewalk and engulfed the librarian's tiny frame in a tender hug.

Reo's heart pounded as she watched a small crowd form around him. Townies who remembered Jack from his high school football days slapped him on the back and shook his hand. Women fluttered around him like hummingbirds, drinking in his all-American good looks. The breath eased out of her lungs. Jack did not intimidate her any more. She didn't care what he thought about her. She'd been in the right at that party. He was the one who'd been out of line.

The town hall clock struck nine. Pushing thoughts of Jack out of her mind, she trotted over to the timekeeper's table, snatched up the results, and hurried to the stage where Mayor Burgin waited. "Here you go!"

The mayor took the results and walked to the podium. Lavinia stood beaming at his side as he began his remarks. The crowd gathered around the stage, faces bright and attentive.

Reo felt a tug on her sleeve. She turned around to see the stooped back of Mrs. Newmacher, motioning for her to follow.

"Would you help me?" Mrs. Newmacher asked over her shoulder as she shuffled towards Sweet Blossoms, her florist shop. Her wrinkled hand brushed the gray bangs out of her eyes. "I want to put out some flower baskets while folks are still milling around. Potential sales, you know."

Reo shot a look at the stage where the mayor was speaking. She wanted to hear him announce the winners, but how could she say no to Mrs. Newmacher? "Sure." She followed the florist into the shop, lifted two of the hanging baskets, and carried them to the sidewalk. Mrs. Newmacher pointed to the hooks where she wanted Reo to hang the pink and white petunias.

"I'll roll out the flower carts after they take down the stage, just like we agreed," Mrs. Newmacher said when they finished hanging half a dozen baskets. She stood back and admired the display. "I don't know why anyone would decorate with balloons or plastic streamers when they could use vibrant, natural blossoms."

Reo glanced at the red, white, and blue balloon arch covering the finish line and frowned. Was Mrs. Newmacher talking about the race decorations? Who ever heard of hanging flowers over a finish line?

The florist turned an admiring eye to her shop window where lush lilac blossoms cascaded from a wicker basket. A heart-shaped lavender sign reminded customers to purchase flowers for Mother's Day. Only one day left.

Reo looked away.

"Flowers make the best decorations, don't you agree?" Mrs. Newmacher asked.

Reo flipped through the papers on her clipboard. "They certainly are pretty."

"Let's have a round of applause for all the volunteers who made this day possible," the mayor said over the loudspeaker. "Special thanks to Reo Greene for taking the lead and making everything run smoothly."

Her cheeks warmed as the folks around her smiled and clapped.

Mrs. Newmacher rested her wrinkled hand on Reo's shoulder. "Thank you for your help, dear." She shuffled back into her shop.

Country music played over the loudspeakers as the mayor left the podium. The high school coaches got to work disassembling the stage and loading the parts into pickup trucks. Reo texted herself a reminder to send thank you notes to the high school band instructor for lending the portable stage and to all the coaches for setting it up and tearing it down. Between finishing her paper, completing her final exams, and preparing for her job interview, her schedule was going to be crazy this week. She'd feel so much better once she got the call from Lilac Mountain High School with her interview time.

"Rhiannon Greene," a female voice boomed over the music. "Drop the clipboard and put your hands up."

Reo whirled around.

Her best friend Sunny DeStefano stood in the middle of Main Street, directing traffic with a megaphone and pointing at her. Wearing an orange construction vest over her swirly pink sun dress, Sunny held up a manicured hand to stop pedestrians as a row of pickup trucks backed into the lane. Once all the trucks pulled away, she waved the pedestrians across the street and scurried to the sidewalk. "Let the traffic begin!" she called through the megaphone, motioning for the waiting cars to move.

"Look at that. Plenty of time before the limo arrives." Sunny fluffed her long dark hair off her shoulders. A single neon-pink-dyed curl curved around her right cheek. "My mom just texted me. She's doing hair at the bride's house. The family's going nuts, worrying the race won't be over in time for the limo to park in front of St. Andrew's."

Reo sank onto a wrought iron bench, overcome with relief as the crowd mingled around them. The race was over. She'd done it. "Thanks for taking charge of clean-up."

"Because I'm so good at ordering people around? One of the secret powers I inherited from my mother." Sunny spread the hem of her skirt and did a mini curtsy before dropping onto the bench. "You had the harder job. Convincing all these Main Street business owners to even have a race. I'd have no patience for that."

"If anyone says another word about blocking ATM access or interfering with yoga studio ambiance, shoot me." Reo fought the wave of exhaustion that washed over her, stifling a yawn. "I barely slept last night, worrying something would go wrong."

"You worry too much." Sunny pulled off the orange construction vest and folded it. "Although my mom did want to call you at five a.m. this morning. She was mad about the race clock being set up in front of the salon. I had to wrestle the phone out of her hand and hide it."

Reo glanced over at the Up Do salon where volunteers were taking down the clock. "Do you think I did okay?"

"Aside from not wearing that cute white denim skirt you bought last week for the race?"

Reo's hand flew to her cheek. "I completely forgot." She glanced down at her oversized Ridgeland College tee shirt, bike shorts, and running shoes. "I got up so early, I pulled on the first thing I saw."

Sunny shrugged. "Considering you spilled water all over the mayor, it's probably good you didn't wear the new skirt."

Reo cringed. "You saw that."

"Couldn't miss it." Sunny's gaze narrowed. "I also saw Jack Warfield bump into you."

Reo crossed her arms, remembering his crack about her attitude. "He's still mad at me."

Sunny snorted. "You'd think he'd be over it by now."

"You'd think." Reo rolled her eyes. "Any idea why the mayor wants to meet with Jack and me Monday morning?"

"Together?" Sunny scrunched up her face then snapped her fingers. "Maybe he wants you two to end your feud."

Reo looked towards the library where a crowd of folks still stood talking with Jack. "There's no feud. He just blames me for destroying his chance to go to college."

"Like he needed help with that." Sunny's phone dinged. She shoved the megaphone into Reo's hands and jumped to her feet. "Mom ran out of hair spray. Are we done?"

Reo glanced around. Runners and spectators mingled around the storefronts, munching on the after-race snacks set out by each shop. The stage was gone. The water tables had been cleared and put away. Traffic was flowing again which meant she could go home and get to work on her paper. She nodded. "The firemen will take down the balloon arch later this evening. Thanks again for helping." She waved to Sunny, then stretched out her legs and yawned. Her first moment of peace since before dawn. The breeze felt so nice. She'd enjoy it for a few minutes and then—

"Reo!" a male voice barked. "What is this mess?"

She jerked up straight and looked around.

Allen Owens of Allen and Eva's Organic Produce stood outside the entrance of his store, his arm extended in a rigid line. Dressed in denim overalls and a plaid shirt, he pointed his index finger at a group of metal folding chairs stacked in front of his strawberry stand. "We talked about this. Our customers must have easy access to the produce at all times."

"The pickup trucks will be back in just a few minutes."

Allen raised his eyebrows and shook his head. "I need these chairs moved now."

"All right." She rose to her feet. So much for relaxing.

~

Jack frowned at the welcome banner. The simple flyer he'd spotted outside the convenience store last night had made the race sound like a community fun run. Just the thing to blow off steam after the week he'd had. No wonder the folks at the registration table had been so friendly when he'd signed in. He'd stumbled when he noticed his name hanging above the finish line, his misstep propelling him straight into Reo Greene.

Now, as a result of that banner announcing his return, a group of residents crowded around him.

"When'd you arrive in town?" a woman standing beside him asked.

He smiled politely. "Last night."

"See any action?" an older gentleman chimed in.

"In Lilac?" Jack deadpanned. "No, sir."

After the laughter died down, another man asked, "Where were you stationed?"

Reminded him of somebody, but darn if he could remember who. "Split my time between the Middle East and Texas."

"Your Texas unit earned the medal for the hostage rescue, right?"

"Yes, sir." Jack nodded.

The man patted him on the back. "Two heroes in one family. Always knew you'd follow in your father's footsteps."

Had the sun on his face gotten hotter? "Just doing my duty." Jack's gaze strayed over the crowd, honed in on Reo, her blond ponytail swaying as she talked on her cell phone. Of all the people he could have collided with, why did it have to be her? Annoyance shot through him as memories of senior year came rushing back. He'd hated her for what she'd done the night of that party. And it was clear from the way she'd pushed out of his arms this morning that she was still angry at him, too.

"When did you get out of the army?" a woman who reminded him of somebody from his mother's former garden club asked.

"Six months ago."

"What're you doing now?" she asked.

"Working in Washington as a conflict mediator." And he'd be doing it right now if he weren't on a leave of absence. Another thing he hadn't seen coming.

"How's your momma doing?" a man asked.

"Very well, sir. She lives with her sister in Tampa. They own a yarn shop."

"What are your plans, son?"

"Right now?" Jack asked. "Get used to being back in Lilac."

"That should take all of ten minutes. Then what?"

"Put my mother's rental property on the market. The tenants moved out and Mom's decided to sell."

"Sell? You're not gonna move in?"

Something pointed poked his palm. A brunette wearing a sleek green dress folded his fingers over a business card. "If you need a real estate agent, you know who to call." She flashed a bright smile at him.

"Yes, ma'am." He'd definitely seen her face before. Wasn't she the mother of one of his high school buddies?

"Been looking for you! There's a '69 Mustang in the shop you've got to see." Pete Warfield sidled into the group and slapped Jack on the back.

Pain shot through his shoulder. Direct hit on the stitches. He flinched as Pete pulled him into a bear hug, exhaling slowly when his uncle released him. Good ol' Pete. His thinning hair seemed grayer, but a good-natured smile still lit up his weathered features. They said their good-byes to the group and headed down the sidewalk.

Pete hitched up his jeans and turned to his nephew as

soon as they were out of ear shot. "Aren't you gonna thank me for rescuing you?"

"Sure. Right after I thank you for telling everyone I was coming back. Not."

"I may have mentioned to Tom Burgin you were coming back. But don't blame me for that banner. That was Lavinia's idea. Tom would have an easier time stopping a speeding locomotive than saying no to Lavinia." Pete shook his head. "The woman would tie bows on every door knob if the town council would let her get away with it."

"So much for slipping quietly into town."

"You think that was even an option? Lavinia wanted to give you a parade." Pete chuckled. "Best to get the welcome home stuff over with as quickly as possible. Like ripping off a bandage."

The men walked out of the bright sun into the cool interior of Warfield's Garage. Jack inhaled the familiar scent of car polish and engine oil. He'd spent countless hours hanging out here as a kid, shooting the breeze with the uncle who'd taught him how to fix a flat and jump-start a battery. He whistled at the sight of the cherry-red convertible. "Sweet."

Pete nodded. "Belongs to one of the managers at the solar plant. Brings it here for tune-ups."

Jack circled the car, drinking in the details. A rich man's toy. "Good choice, since you're old enough to remember when the original model came out," he said with a grin.

Pete rested his hand on the hood. "They don't make 'em like they used to. Cars or men."

What did that mean? "Business must be good at the plant," Jack continued. "None of the guys I grew up with could afford a vehicle like this."

"No kidding."

"Any idea why Mayor Burgin wants to see me and Reo Greene in his office Monday morning?"

"You *and* Reo?" Pete's brows shot up. He rubbed the back of his neck. "The mayor might've said something about an opening on the town council."

Jack snorted. "Nice try. Told you. I'm not moving back to Lilac."

Pete fixed him with a serious look. "Your mother thinks you're risking your life for people who don't even want your help."

Jack stared at the grease-stained concrete floor and counted to ten. His mother had made it perfectly clear she thought he was wasting his talents working as a Peacetalkers' mediator. "If everyone believed that, all the violence in the world would never stop. You agree with her?"

"Don't know much about big city gangs," Pete said. "Just think it would be nice for you to come home. Take over the garage so it stays in the family."

Jack leaned a hip against the worktable. "Should've thought about that before you became a confirmed bachelor."

Pete's eyes flashed. He pointed at the sepia-toned photograph on the wall. "Your Great-Grandpa Warfield built this garage almost a century ago. Doesn't that mean anything to you?" He shook his head, his expression disappointed. "Had the same conversation with your father."

And if he'd listened, he might still be alive. His father had wanted nothing to do with the family business. He'd joined the army, chased adventure, and died a hero. "I gotta go. Get out of these sweaty clothes."

Pete turned away, busied himself rearranging the tools on his worktable. The whir of the overhead fan filled the awkward silence.

Jack blew out a breath. "How about breakfast tomorrow?"

"Yeah, sure." Pete didn't look up.

Jack pushed his hair out of his eyes. He'd pissed off his uncle, been lassoed by the mayor for some mysterious project, and collided with the one girl who despised him. Maybe hunkering down in Lilac until this leave of absence business blew over wasn't the best plan of action after all.

Chapter Two

Reo awoke with her arms wrapped around a mountain of pillows. Sunlight slanted through the mini blinds, striping the pale purple carpet that had covered her bedroom floor since her fourteenth birthday. She rolled onto her back and stretched her arms over her head then quickly tucked them under the down quilt. Spring may have come to Lilac, but the mountain town remained stubbornly chilly at night.

A gentle knock sounded.

"Reo?" Donnie Greene opened his daughter's bedroom door a crack. "You awake?"

"Uh-huh." She ran a hand through her tousled hair. An open laptop sat at the foot of her bed. How late had she stayed up working on that paper? She'd been so tired when she'd finished returning all the folding chairs to the high school yesterday that she'd come home and collapsed onto her bed, waking after dinnertime to work on her research paper.

"Heading off to church in a bit. You coming?"

Donnie's tall frame filled the doorway, his dark hair neatly combed into place. He wore the same navy blue suit he wore every Sunday, his posture the straightest she'd seen since the bus accident. The doctors said her father had fully recovered, but she still saw the occasional uneven hunch of his shoulders, the slight drag of his right foot.

She reached for her laptop. "I have to finish this assignment. It's due tomorrow."

Donnie hesitated a moment, then nodded. "Might be going out to eat or fishing with Pete this afternoon. The house'll be quiet."

"Thanks," she answered without looking up, her fingers busy typing. After the door clicked shut, she pushed the laptop away and fell back onto the pillows.

You understand, don't you, God?

She stared at the ceiling. Mother's Day had been tolerable while Granny Greene had been alive. She and Dad used to spend the entire day with her grandmother, starting with church and ending with Dad grilling everyone's favorite barbequed chicken in the back yard. But Granny Greene had died two years ago, and that first Mother's Day without her had been awful.

She flipped onto her stomach. She didn't like to think about her mother. Carly Day was the beautiful woman her father had married, the woman who'd given her life, so she supposed she was grateful for that. But the rest of it—her mother's dramatic departure with a visiting British professor, the awkward contacts afterwards—she preferred to keep those memories locked in a box where they belonged. She'd accepted her mother was incapable of settling down and thanked God she wasn't like her. She'd learned to control her own impulsiveness since the night of Jack's last high school party and was a better person because of it.

The faint scent of cilantro and onions suddenly tickled her nostrils. Her head popped up at the sound of clattering dishes. She kicked off the blanket and bolted out of bed. Gina was back.

After pulling on jeans and a worn Lilac Mountain High School sweatshirt, she hurried down the hall to the kitchen. Her sixteen-year-old half-sister Gina stood in front of the stove, all four-feet-ten inches of her, scrambling eggs with the ease of a natural-born chef. People said the two didn't look anything alike, that Reo had their mother's blue eyes and blond hair while Gina had her own father's dark hair and olive skin. Yet when Gina stood in front of the stove, one hand on her hip, head tilted confidently to the side, she resembled their mother Carly Day more than Reo ever would.

Gina grinned. "Donnie said you were too tired to go to church, so I'm cooking us breakfast."

"Thank you!" Reo hugged her sister's slender shoulders. "How was Virginia Beach? I saw the pictures you posted."

"Fun. My aunt showed me how to make breakfast burritos." Gina slid a warmed tortilla onto a plate, laid on a grilled ham slice and scrambled eggs, and rolled it up. "Here you go."

Reo sat at the table and took a bite, savoring every flavor. "How do you make simple ingredients taste so good?" The quality of the meals in the Greene home went up a hundred percent whenever Gina dropped in for a visit. "You could do this for a living."

"Papa says I get it from his grandfather who was a great *cocinero*." She poured them both a glass of juice and sat down. "You don't look so good. Are you okay?"

"Just tired from the 5K race yesterday." Reo swallowed the delicious food. "Jack Warfield's back in town."

Gina's eyes widened. "The guy you called the cops on? Oh, my God, he's so hot!"

Reo choked on her food. Gina hurried around the table and pounded her back.

"How do you know what he looks like?" Reo croaked, sipping her juice. "You were little back then." Plus, Gina lived with her father twenty miles away in Carsondale.

"You showed me his yearbook picture. And I saw him once outside Warfield's Garage. Does he have a girlfriend?"

"How should I know?" Reo clutched a crumpled paper napkin in her fist as she continued to eat her food in silence. She'd never told anyone about her high school crush on Jack. People had felt sorry enough for her as a kid, the way Carly Day had run off. If they'd known she'd had feelings for the town partier, she'd have been the object of outright pity.

Gina rested her chin on her hand, her expression curious. "What exactly did he do to you again?"

Reo swallowed the last bite. "He threw me out of his party."

Gina's jaw dropped. "No way! What did you do?"

Reo slammed down her fork. "What did I do? I didn't do anything!" She crossed her arms, the memory of that night making her blood rush. "One minute I was climbing up the fire escape with everyone else. The next minute he was dragging me downstairs and telling me to go home.”

“Wait!” Gina clutched her arm. “Climbing up *what* fire escape?”

“Jack lived in the apartment over Warfield’s Garage during senior year. He had these parties. Kids would sneak out after their parents went to bed.”

“In Lilac? He didn’t get caught?”

Reo’s face burned. “Well, he did after I called the cops, which I wouldn’t have done if he hadn’t—” She jumped to her feet. “Hey, let’s drive to the overlook.”

“If he hadn’t what?” Gina asked.

Kissed her like nobody had before or since. Just the memory of it made Reo’s entire body tingle. She carried her plate to the sink and scrubbed it clean. “Dad and I used to take Granny Greene to the scenic overlook every Mother’s Day.” She sloshed water onto the floor and scowled.

Gina laughed. “Hey, don’t change the subject. I want to hear more about Jack.” She checked her phone. “I can stay until two. Felipe is picking me up after he eats brunch with his mom.”

Felipe? She hadn’t heard Gina mention that name before. A new boyfriend? “Did Felipe drop you off here?”

Gina nodded. “We’re going off-roading later.”

“Does he go to school with you?” Reo glanced over her shoulder as she retrieved her purse from the hook near the kitchen door.

“He graduated last year. He works for Papa mowing lawns.”

Felipe had his diploma and a job. She exhaled a sigh of relief. The last boy Gina had been interested in had dropped out of school at age fifteen and hadn’t been able to find work anywhere.

Reo drove them in her old Ford compact up the winding mountain road. The engine whined as they climbed around the bend. Should she ask Gina more about Felipe? She glanced in the rearview mirror. Maybe if she didn't ask Gina about Felipe, Gina wouldn't ask her about Jack.

"Oh, how cool," Gina exclaimed as they cruised up the lilac-lined road to the overlook. Pink, purple, and white blossoms burst from the lush green bushes, creating a vibrant border for the scenic mountain byway. "I've got to tell Felipe about this." She tapped her phone and started texting.

Reo parked in the empty gravel lot and climbed out of the car, inhaling the fresh mountain air. What was it about Lilac Mountain that made her feel so peaceful? She pulled out her phone, angling the lens so that lush blossoms framed the image of the town below, and snapped a couple pictures. After selecting the best one, she uploaded it to the Lilac social media page with the caption, *Live from the Scenic Overlook.*

Gina plopped onto the bench and stared into the distance. "Maria is pregnant again."

"You don't sound excited." Reo sat beside her. It was no secret Gina couldn't stand her father's second wife.

"Papa is making a big deal about it. Taking her and Alejandro out to lunch after church."

"You didn't want to go?"

Gina shook her head. "She's not my mother. All she wants me to do is babysit Alejandro. Papa says I have to help as long as I live under his roof. I can't wait until I graduate."

Reo had no idea what it was like to live with a stepmother since her own father had never remarried. She slid an arm around Gina's shoulders. "Maria isn't mean to you, is she?" she asked.

"Nothing I do makes her happy." Gina dug the toe of her sneaker into the dirt. "Do you think our mom ever thinks about us?"

Reo's heart squeezed. "I don't know." Resentment seethed inside her. How could their mother have been so unfeeling! Even though Gina was younger, she'd spent more years with Carly Day than Reo had, which meant more memories, more sadness when she left. "You know, you can move in with my dad and me anytime."

"I know. But I'd have to transfer schools." Gina rested her head on Reo's shoulder. "I'd drop out now if I could."

"Gina!"

"What? I hate school. I'm not learning anything useful."

"You liked it when I was doing my student teaching at Carsondale High last fall." Even though Gina hadn't been a student in Reo's class, they had seen each other frequently during the day. She'd always appeared happy.

Gina stared at the ground.

"Don't you want to go to college?" Reo pressed.

"More school? No way. You've been going to college forever."

Reo's face warmed. "That's because I kept changing my major."

"I thought you wanted to be a nurse."

"I did, but I failed anatomy. Then I switched to

accounting, but it was really boring. Now I'm majoring in education and I love it. Plus, most of the classes are online."

"When do you graduate?" Gina asked.

"In August." Reo sighed. She should be graduating in May. Things had been so hectic at course registration time, between student teaching and organizing the 5K. She'd been positive she knew exactly what classes she needed to take to finish her degree. By the time she'd realized she hadn't registered for one course she needed, the spring class was filled. She had to register for the June offering, delaying her graduation until the end of the summer.

"How can you afford all the tuition?" Gina asked. "Papa says we don't have the money."

"I qualify for scholarships. And you would, too. Hey, what about culinary school? You'd be a great chef."

Gina shrugged. "I don't know."

Reo gave her shoulders a squeeze. "I'll be interviewing soon for a teaching job at Lilac Mountain High. If you move to Lilac and I get hired, we could be together for your senior year. Wouldn't that be great?"

"It's still school." Gina kicked at the dirt.

A horn sounded. Reo glanced around to see a black Jeep driven by a handsome young man with a bright smile and dark hair. The jeep pulled up right behind the bench, spewing gravel as it stopped.

"Felipe!" Gina jumped to her feet, her expression bright. "Reo, this is Felipe. Felipe, this is Reo."

Felipe waved at Reo and flashed a grin at Gina. "We finished brunch early. Ready?"

Gina looked over her shoulder. "Okay if I leave you

here?"

Reo wanted to talk more about the importance of staying in school, but it looked like now wasn't the time. "Sure. I need to head back and work on my paper." She gave Gina a hug. "Thanks for cooking breakfast."

Gina ran to the passenger side and climbed in. "See you later."

Reo watched as they drove away, then wandered to the overlook platform. The town of Lilac sat nestled below, bordered on one side by the railroad tracks and the other by the meandering Cool Water Run. She shaded her eyes with her hand. If she squinted she could just make out the front of The Shoebox Diner. Was Dad there having lunch with Pete? Probably a lot of the town's mothers were there, celebrating with their families.

She gripped the railing. Her own mother had given birth to five children by five different men. Beautiful and wild, Carly Day captured the attention of every man she met then disappeared as soon as things got boring.

She was twenty-three. It shouldn't hurt so much.

Thank goodness her own father was reliable. He'd let Carly Day divorce him, but insisted on keeping Reo in Lilac to raise her. She blinked, remembering last year, that first Mother's Day after Granny Greene's death. Right in the middle of church, tears had sprung into Reo's eyes without warning, spilling down her cheeks. She'd hurried out of the service into the ladies' room, hiding in a stall while she struggled to muffle her sobs. After washing her face, she'd told the concerned women who'd gathered that she'd been crying for her grandmother. And Granny Greene's death had certainly been part of Reo's churning emotions. But deep down there was something else, something sad and unspoken, threatening to unsettle her otherwise cheerful nature without a moment's notice. Most days she could keep those memories of her mother locked up.

Just not on Mother's Day.

She took a deep breath as her gaze followed the hiking trail that wound from Lilac's municipal park up to the overlook. Didn't appear to be anybody hiking today. No, wait. Someone was walking on the trail, not far below her. Reo's eyes widened with recognition as the breeze blew chestnut hair across the hiker's sunglasses.

She heard the soft sound of fluttering wings emanating from her phone.

It couldn't be.

She stood in shock, listening, as the identical fluttering sound echoed from the hiking trail below.

She watched in disbelief as Jack glanced at his phone and smiled.

That app hadn't made a peep on her phone in over five years. Now it jolted her phone awake with the image of flapping silver wings above a name.

Jack3387.

Jack squinted at his phone. "Reo12. How'd you get only two digits?" He climbed onto the platform beside her, his chiseled face wet with perspiration. "Guess Reo must be a really unique name."

"What are you doing with that app?" Her gaze riveted to his sweat-drenched face, she took a step backwards. Did that app even have a name? She'd been given it for performing a good deed without being asked. What was it doing on Jack's phone?

"I could ask you the same question." He took off his sunglasses and swiped a muscled arm across his forehead. "You look like you're thinking the same thing I thought when I chased down a kid for stealing a lady's purse. When I caught him, the app went off on both of our phones."

She sidestepped, putting the bench between them. Her heart pounded as she watched him drain his bottle of water.

"It's customary to tell the story of how you got the app when you make a new acquaintance who has it." He cocked his brow, waiting.

"You're not a new acquaintance. And nobody ever told me that." Her thoughts raced as she gripped the back of the bench. Jack was the last person she'd share her story with. Yet he had the app. What the heck?

When she didn't respond, he settled his elbows against the overlook railing and leaned back. "My buddy Steve gave me the app when I helped him prepare for a fitness test. We served in the army together. Very by-the-book kind of guy. You'd like him."

She narrowed her gaze. "What's that supposed to mean?"

His glance cut straight through her. "You follow the rules. You've always followed the rules."

"And you like to break them." She thrust her hands into her pockets, irritated he could sum up her behavior so easily.

For a second it looked like he flinched. "Anyway, five minutes after we met, Steve could see my life was a mess. Anger issues. Counseling sessions. I mean, heck, I was marching around some desert on a mission I didn't give a darn about. The way I saw it, I was supposed to be attending a big university on a football scholarship."

Her gaze flew to his face. The mix of anger and regret she saw there tugged at something inside her. She lifted her chin. "And you blamed me."

"I realized that's what you thought when I ran into you yesterday."

His athletic physique exuded the silent power of muscles held in check. Reo's mouth suddenly felt dry. He was in even better shape now than when he had played football.

Jack slipped on his sunglasses. "If I were still angry about you calling the cops, I would've done a lot more than run into you."

His confession reverberating in the air around her. She watched, dumbfounded, as he descended the platform steps.

~

"See you in the mayor's office," he called over his shoulder as he descended the trail. "You owe me a story."

The sun slid behind a puffy white cloud, casting shadows over the lilac blossoms. Jack chuckled to himself. That expression on Reo's face. Priceless. He'd gotten over losing the football scholarship. Eventually. But if he hadn't, her reaction at seeing him just now would have been more than enough payback. For a moment, it looked like she was going to bolt for her car. Did she really think he wanted revenge?

He glanced again at the wings flapping on his phone. The app hadn't gone off once since his return to Lilac.

Where had Reo gotten it?

Reo12. She was unique for more than just her name. He'd intimidated criminals twice her size with a single glare, yet she'd stood her ground, unflinching. She had guts.

Of course, she'd already proven her courage years ago by calling the cops on him. What high school kid in her right mind would shut down a party with free beer?

His cell phone rang. Steve. Sunday afternoon calls from the boss were never good. "Checking up on me?"

"Finished selling that house?" Steve asked. His boss was nothing if not direct.

"Not even on the market yet." Jack stretched his back, wincing as pain shot through his shoulder. "Don't tell me. Peacetalkers has suspended my suspension."

Silence. "Actually, they just launched a formal investigation."

Jack nearly dropped his phone. "What?"

"The goal of our work is to prevent violence," Steve said, his tone serious. "When injuries occur, there are all kinds of questions."

"But I was meeting with Marco on my own time," Jack protested. "Not as a Peacetalker."

"That's another thing." Steve raised his voice. "You violated Peacetalker policy when you did that."

"I can't meet with gang members as a private citizen?"

"No, you can't. It's just like the army. You don't stop being a soldier when you go home for dinner." Steve paused, as if he were trying to get his exasperation under control. "You're supposed to be familiar with all the policies. As a Peacetalker, you represent something bigger than yourself."

Jack stared at the pebbled trail beneath his feet. "Was that in the fine print I signed?"

Steve didn't laugh at his lame attempt at humor. "You're in the first-year probationary period. They have to evaluate everything you do to make sure you're ready to be a Peacetalker." Steve paused. "Did you drink alcohol before you met with Marco?"

Jack gripped the phone tight as he picked up his pace. "You know I don't drink anymore."

"I know, but I had to ask. They're going to ask that and a whole lot more if they bring you in for a formal hearing."

This was serious.

The sound of laughter broke the silence. A hundred yards or so below him, the trail ended in Lilac's municipal park. Little kids ran joyously around the jungle gym. Others soared high on swings, their parents pushing them. Still others enjoyed the warm weather on blankets, cradling babies and sharing a picnic lunch.

"Patti wants to know how your shoulder is," Steve said, his tone back to normal.

Jack slowed to an easy stroll. "Tell her it's almost healed. How's Steve Junior?"

"ETA on track for Labor Day." His voice was filled with anticipation.

"Is that a joke?" Jack asked.

Steve chuckled. "You still want to be the godfather?"

"Shouldn't you wait until after the investigation?" Jack's voice sounded more defensive than he'd intended.

"That's what I was thinking," Steve said. "Just kidding."

Jack's jaw muscles eased. "Tell Patti 'Happy Almost

Mother's Day' for me."

"Will do."

As Jack hung up, his gaze moved to the tiny pair of wings flapping in the corner of the phone's display. He tapped them.

Be not afraid.

He reread the inspirational message that appeared on the screen. The tension drained out of him as he resumed walking. The app's words of hope were randomly generated. He knew that. But couldn't they also be a sign that he was meant to be a member of Peacetalkers? Steve had joined the group after getting out of the army and had put in a good word for Jack, explaining how their unit had negotiated the release of hostages. The Peacetalkers then reached out and invited him to interview. They'd said it took special skills to facilitate communication between people whose primary goal in life was to kill each other. He'd jumped at the chance to negotiate peace between rival urban gangs. It was what he was meant to do with his life, he was sure of it.

But negotiating peace in an urban setting was not the same as rescuing hostages in a war zone. There were different rules now. He needed to remember that.

Chapter Three

Reo searched through her makeup case as the Monday morning sun reflected in the mirror above the bathroom sink. Where was that concealer? She wouldn't have needed it if she hadn't stayed up past midnight to complete her research paper. But it was finished and submitted, thank God. Now all she had left were two final exams. And one four-week summer class. And her job interview. Lilac Mountain High should be calling her any day now to set it up.

The kitchen timer dinged just as she finished tucking the hem of her pink blouse into her black pencil skirt. Dressier clothes than she usually wore to her job at the DMV, but she was meeting with the mayor.

And Jack.

She brushed her hair off her shoulders. Who did he think he was, telling her she owed him a story. She did not owe Jack Warfield anything. He and his friends had made her senior year miserable after she'd called the cops. That flapping wings app going off when they were together didn't mean anything.

She hurried to the kitchen to check the spinach lasagna she'd popped into the oven for her father's lunch. Ten forty-five. Where was Dad? Had something happened on his school bus route? Road crews were repaving the highway. Did he get caught in traffic? She nibbled her bottom lip. He was always home by now.

She pulled out her phone and tapped the local traffic app. No accidents. He was just late. She dropped into a chair and opened her social media news feed, scanning the comments former Lilac residents had posted about the town's first 5K race.

Didn't know there was enough paved road for a 5K race.

Where did all those people come from?

Lilac races into 21ˢᵗ century. About time!

She heard the familiar stomp of her father's boots up the porch steps and threw open the screen door. "There you are."

Donnie smiled. "Don't tell me you were worried."

"Maybe about the casserole in the oven." She reached for her purse. "Five more minutes and it comes out—unless you want a burned lunch."

"You do too much. Other girls your age—"

Not this conversation again. "Are out partying and living the wild life? I told you to stop watching reality TV."

He hung his jacket on a hook and sat. "I was going to say other girls your age are moving to the city or traveling."

She rolled her eyes. "And where would I go? Run off to chase the next big adventure?"

Her father's expression fell.

She regretted the words as soon as they were out of her mouth. She hadn't mentioned her mother's name, but she might as well have. Even now, after all these years, she could tell the thought of Carly Day's running off still got to Dad.

She put her hands on her hips. "If you don't stop saying things like that, I'll start thinking you want to get rid of me. Now if you'll excuse me, I have to see what the mayor wants and then go help all the unhappy people standing in line at the DMV."

"About the DMV—"

She kissed his cheek. "Can it wait until I get back? My meeting's at eleven and I don't want to be late."

He nodded. "Sure. See you tonight."

She ran outside to her car, backed out of the driveway, and drove to Main Street. Of course, there were no open spaces. She swung into the alley beside the Up Do salon and parked.

A swirl of yellow appeared as she hurried past the salon entrance. Sunny stood in the open door. "Wait!" she called.

"Can't. I'm late," Reo replied as she continued past, her steps brisk. "Text me."

Sunny ran along beside her, stiletto heels clacking on the pavement as she fumbled with the clasp of her necklace. "Stop. Turn around." She took the silver necklace from her neck and put it around Reo's. "There. Your neckline needed something."

"Fashionista!" Leave it to Sunny. Reo waved her thanks, continuing past Sparkles Galore and up the block to the town hall. Whatever the mayor wanted had better not be something as time-consuming as a 5K race. She'd already told Leanne Killian, her boss at the

DMV, that she would increase her part-time hours for the summer once her final exams were over. Not to mention Miss Emma had asked her to help with weekly story time at the library since the assistant librarian had gone out on maternity leave. And she'd promised the Girl Scout troop she would participate in a quilting bee to help them finish the commemorative quilt they were making for Lilac's upcoming two-hundred-fiftieth anniversary celebration.

She passed the purple-and-yellow pansy-lined border of the town square. Any day now she should be getting a call to schedule her job interview at the high school. While a few of the students in her teaching degree program were looking for positions in cities, it seemed like more of them wanted to teach in small towns. Like Reo, they'd enjoyed their student teaching experiences in the schools surrounding Ridgeland College and wanted to stay on Lilac Mountain.

She pulled open the door to the town hall and hurried through the lobby to the mayor's office. Mayor Burgin sat at his desk, reading a paper. Jack sat in the chair facing the desk, but his head was turned. He stared out the window, his profile grim.

The mayor motioned her into the room. "There you are. Please sit down."

She took the seat next to Jack. In his khaki slacks and blue button-down shirt, he looked very professional. His hands clutched some papers. He glanced at her briefly, then turned his head again to stare out the window.

She felt like she'd just walked into a funeral parlor. Why wasn't anybody smiling?

The mayor pushed aside the paper he'd been reading.

"I'm sure you've been wondering why I wanted to see the two of you."

She nodded.

"I need your help with a small project." The mayor handed her a stapled report that looked identical to the papers Jack held in his hands.

She glanced at the title page. *Main Street Decoration Proposals for Lilac's 250th Anniversary Celebration.* "You want us to help decorate Main Street?"

The mayor shook his head, his expression solemn. "If it were only that easy. Go ahead and look it over. You'll see three very different proposals for how we should decorate Main Street. Even though the anniversary is two years away, we need to make decisions about the decorations now."

She flipped through the pages. A proposal from Mrs. Newmacher to decorate every Main Street shop window with lilacs. Another from Allen and Eva's Organic Produce proposing a harvest theme. And Lavinia Burgin wanted the entire town draped in patriotic streamers and bunting.

She gulped and looked up.

"You can see my predicament. The celebration is scheduled for September twenty-first, the day Scottish botanist Hamish McPhee founded the town. Unfortunately, Lilacs bloom in the spring, so any lilacs Erin Newmacher uses would have to be grown in hot houses at triple the price. Allen Owens is focused on the harvest season, but will be accused by other business owners of trying to increase his produce sales. And, of course, if I select my wife's suggestion, folks'll cry favoritism."

And if he doesn't pick Lavinia's, his life will be

miserable. "What about the town council members?" she asked. "Why can't they pick one?"

"Everyone on the town council has an existing personal or business relationship with the folks who submitted the proposals." He cleared his throat. "What I need is an impartial team to evaluate these proposals and reach a consensus with the Main Street business owners before our next town council meeting."

"That's next week," she blurted. "It took months to get all the business owners to agree to the 5K race." Who would've thought the yoga school would be the final holdout to give approval for a healthy activity like a race?

"But the point is, you did it." The mayor gave her a pointed look. "I need you to do it again."

It was true. She knew everyone's concerns about the 5K race. And the issues they'd had with race day might not be too different from the issues they would have with the town's anniversary celebration. With luck, she could wrap this up before her summer class started. "I'll talk to them."

The mayor nodded, his expression pleased. "I want you two to do it together."

She waved her hand, dismissive. "Honestly, I don't need Jack to get this done. No offense, Jack, but you've been gone for five years. You'd just be in the way."

The corner of Jack's mouth curved. "Nice try."

Mayor Burgin leaned back in his chair. "I take it you don't know what Jack does for a living."

Her brow crinkled. "Um, no."

"He's an urban crisis mediator."

Her gaze flew to Jack's face. "What?"

"Surprise." He gave her a dry look.

With the physique he had, she'd assumed he was a football coach or maybe a personal trainer. An urban crisis mediator. "Well, then," she offered, as the glimmer of an idea formed. "Perhaps Jack can do this job without me."

The mayor shook his head. "It has to be both of you."

"Why?" she exclaimed. "It doesn't make sense to force Jack to work with me if he's not interested. And if he's a trained negotiator, he doesn't need me."

The mayor leaned forward, arms crossed on his desk. "I want to make an example of you two."

Reo's eyes flew wide. "What?"

"Everyone knows you don't get along. If you two can work together, then the Main Street business owners should be willing to work together, too."

She crossed her legs, her thoughts racing as her foot bobbed up and down. She couldn't fault his logic. Lord knows everything would go smoother in Lilac if everyone cooperated more. The image of the app's silver flapping wings popped into her head. She shot Jack a sideways glance. "What if we didn't hate each other?"

Jack's gaze swung to her face, the first look of interest she'd gotten out of those stony features since she'd entered the mayor's office.

"Jack and I talked yesterday," she continued hastily. "We've decided to let bygones be bygones, haven't we?"

He studied her face for a long moment, his eyes narrowing.

She held his gaze, willing him to remember the olive branch he'd offered her yesterday and to forget the fact that she'd stomped it into the ground.

"Yes, we have," he said finally.

She exhaled her relief.

"That does throw a wrench into things." The mayor tapped his pursed lips. "It's important for people to believe you two still dislike each other and have decided to put aside your disagreement for the good of the town. How difficult would it be to keep your reconciliation a secret? There is something bigger at stake."

She rolled her eyes. Something bigger. Like maybe an election coming up and the mayor not wanting to be accused of favoritism? She searched Jack's face. "Are you willing to do this?"

Jack rolled the report into a tight baton and tapped it against his palm. "As long as we finish quickly. I could be called back to work at any time." He gave the mayor a pointed look.

The mayor rose to his feet and extended his hand to Jack. "Then we understand each other."

Jack shook his hand. "We do."

The mayor's expression relaxed into a satisfied smile. "Thank you once again for stepping up and helping our town. I don't know what we'd do without you. I'm looking forward to hearing what you two come up with."

She walked across the lobby with Jack, their footsteps echoing on the marble. What just happened? Whatever she'd imagined the mayor would be asking them, it wasn't that. They stepped outside. Main Street's shop fronts stretched before them, glistening in the warm midday sun. Shiny new cars shared the parking spaces with rusty pickups. Shoppers walked in and out of stores, carrying their purchases. Folks sat on benches, chatting.

"Hard to believe this sleepy town is a hotbed of discontent," Jack muttered, slipping on his sunglasses.

She bristled at his mocking tone. "You'd have a different opinion if you'd stuck around."

"And done what? Worked in Pete's garage?" His voice sounded bitter.

Did he hate Lilac that much? "Then why did you come back?"

"To get my mother's rental property ready to sell." He jerked his thumb over his shoulder. "That conversation's making me wish she'd hired a contractor. The sooner we get this task done for the mayor, the sooner I'm out of here."

His words stung. "If you're so eager to leave, why did you agree to help?" she asked.

The aroma of coffee and cinnamon popovers drifted through the air. He stopped at the entrance to The Shoebox Diner. "We need to read over the proposals. Let's get something to eat."

"Work here?" She looked through the window at the lunchtime crowd. "I thought maybe the library."

"The mayor wants to make an example of us. Can you think of a better place to start?" The corner of his mouth curved devilishly as he held the door open, head cocked to the side, daring her. As she walked past, he bent his head close to hers. "If we're going to do this, we might as well have some fun," he said softly.

The whisper of his words against her hair sent shivers down her neck. She glanced over her shoulder. He looked like a fox assessing the best way to raid a hen house. *What was he up to?*

The hum of conversation filled the air. Lunchtime regulars filled the booths and perched on stools at the counter.

"Jack Warfield! Wondered when you'd get around to visiting me." Lulu Abernathy set down a steaming carafe of coffee and stomped to the door to greet them. She threw her sturdy arms around his shoulders and pulled him into a bear hug. Her short brown curls stuck out at all angles under her robin's egg blue Shoebox Diner waitress cap as her laughing green eyes flew back and forth between them. "The devil must be ice skating today." She elbowed Reo. "Does being a decorated veteran bring him up to your standards now, young lady?"

Reo eyed Jack up and down. "Too soon to tell. My standards are pretty high."

Jack rested his hand lightly on Reo's back as Lulu led them to their seats. She tried to ignore the warm sensation spreading across her skin. She slid into the red vinyl booth and set the papers on the table.

Jack cleared his throat. "Mayor Burgin asked Reo and me to evaluate the Main Street decoration proposals for the two-hundred-fiftieth anniversary," he said in a voice loud enough for everyone in the diner to hear. "What are your thoughts on that?"

"The two of you working together, or the decoration proposals? Both'll guarantee fireworks." She slapped her thigh, cackling at her joke as she stomped away to greet the next customers.

Reo flipped open the menu with a rigid motion, trying to ignore Lulu's laughter. She looked up and saw Jack smirking at her. "What?"

"High standards, huh?" He slid across the banquette

to face her. "Not too high to climb up my fire escape."

She sniffed. "One impulsive act. I learned my lesson when you threw me out."

He fixed her with a serious look. "You can thank Pete for that."

"Your uncle wasn't there. What did he have to do with it?"

"He told me, and I quote, 'Donnie Greene's daughter is off limits'."

She cocked her head. "Then what would you call that kiss?" She didn't like it one bit that her body still warmed at the memory of his lips on hers.

"Teenage entitlement. After all, you came to me." He spread his arms along the back of the bench, his expression arrogant as he raked her with an assessing gaze. "From what I remember, you liked it."

"Of all the conceited—"

He tapped his chin. "Or have I got that wrong?"

"—egotistical—"

He looked upward as if he were struggling to remember. "Maybe it was that other blond. The cheerleader. What was her name?"

She slammed the menu shut and scrambled across the banquette to leave.

Jack's hand shot out and circled her wrist. "Are we having fun yet?"

His mocking gaze seared her with his intent. She glanced over and saw Lulu watching them along with the lunch counter customers. "I hate you," she hissed. She pulled her wrist free and slid back into place.

"That little performance should be all over town by dinnertime. Exactly what the mayor ordered." He opened the menu with a carefree flip. "Always loved

Lulu's meatloaf. You?"

She glared at him. "Is this what you do as a crisis negotiator? Start fights?"

"Probing for sensitive subjects is part of the negotiation process. We try to avoid fights."

"Let me guess. You have a hard time with that part." She batted her lashes at him.

He flipped the menu page with a jerk of his hand and didn't look up.

Jack was a crisis mediator. How had somebody so impulsive gotten into that line of work? She stole a few discreet glances at his broad shoulders and strong jaw. She still thought he looked more like a professional weight lifter.

After Lulu took their orders and brought the food, they read the Main Street decoration proposals in silence. "In terms of price," Jack said finally, "Lavinia's patriotic banners are the least expensive. But I'll give it to Allen. He has an interesting idea, leveraging crops grown locally."

She waved her salad fork at him. "Don't forget all the other businesses on Main Street. The yoga studio. The bank. Their businesses don't relate directly to the harvest. They might be just as happy with lilacs."

"Not Filmore Hardware. They sell tractors and trowels. I'm guessing they'd be in the harvest camp." He glanced across the street. "How well do you know Allen Owens?"

She dabbed her lips. "Pretty well. His uncle became principal at Lilac Mountain High last year."

"Dave Owens, the math teacher?" Jack made a face. "I hated his algebra class."

"Only algebra? Well, he's a very good principal. I

knew Allen Owens' younger brother Steve a little better. Remember him? He was a couple years behind us." She rested her chin in her hand, forefinger tapping her cheek. "Didn't he go on to play football at the University of Georgia?"

Jack swallowed the last of his meatloaf. "Texas."

"That's right. Texas. What position did he play?"

"Cornerback."

She tilted her head. "Quarterback?"

"No, cornerback."

"Isn't that the position you played?"

He wiped his lips with his napkin. "No, I was fullback."

"Aren't they the same thing?"

"No, they're not. And stop trying to bait me." He slid his plate aside. "You may not be over getting kicked out of my party, but I'm definitely over getting kicked off the football team."

She straightened. "Actually, I was trying to remember if Steve Owens was one of the guys who let the air out of my tires." She watched Jack's eyes widen. "Or maybe he was the one who emptied the recycle bin in front of my locker."

Jack's jaw dropped.

"I know." She snapped her fingers. "I bet he was the one who destroyed my honors biology project." She forced a smile. "Hard to keep track, you turned so many people against me."

She tossed some bills on the table. "Are we having fun yet?"

She didn't wait to hear Jack's response. She slid smoothly out of the booth and waved to Lulu on her way out. "Delicious as always."

Reo strode outside, laughing to herself. Served Jack right for teasing her. Plus, he'd never apologized for any of the pranks she'd endured after the police shutdown his party. Let him stew on that.

She glanced at her phone. Darn. No time to retrieve her car and drive to work. If she walked fast, she'd just make it to the DMV on time. Leanne had been lecturing everyone about being late, and Reo was in no mood for another lecture.

She picked up her pace as she passed the high school. She'd completely overlooked the significance of Allen Owens being related to the principal. Did Principal Owens care if she picked his nephew's harvest proposal? The thought nagged at her as she hurried across the crowded Department of Motor Vehicles parking lot. She rushed through the employee entrance at the stroke of one.

Her boss Leanne stood just inside the door, hands on her hips. Dressed in a tailored mauve suit and matching shoes, she managed the DMV customer service employees with a firm hand. "Reo, we've been over this. I need you to arrive a couple minutes early to stow your things so I can go over instructions."

Reo jammed her time card into the punch clock, then shoved her purse into a locker and turned the key. "I'm sorry. It's been a crazy morning. First my dad came home late, then I had to meet with the mayor."

"Is he all right?" Leanne asked, her voice going up an octave.

Reo slid the locker key into her pocket. "Who? The mayor?"

"No, your dad." Leanne cleared her throat. "I mean, he had that bus accident last year."

"That's so sweet of you to worry." She gripped Leanne's hand and squeezed it. "He's fine."

For a minute it looked like Leanne was going to say something more. Instead, she smoothed her skirt and motioned for Reo to follow.

Reo walked into the main lobby and cringed. The line of customers snaked back and forth through the stanchions all the way to the front door. "I'm so sorry."

Leanne patted her arm. "Just try to arrive when I need you."

"I will." Reo took her place behind the row of terminals at the Information Desk. She needed to arrive on time if she was going to ask Leanne to write her a character reference for her teaching job. And she did not want to anger residents of Lilac and jeopardize her chance of getting hired at Lilac Mountain High by picking the wrong decoration proposal. No matter how Jack treated this assignment, she needed to consider each proposal thoroughly and pick the best one.

She flipped on her Open light and greeted the next customer in line. "May I help you?"

~

"Anything else?" Lulu held a steaming carafe in one hand and a pitcher of iced tea in the other.

Jack set down the proposal he'd just finished reading and inched his mug forward, still trying to figure out what had just happened. How had he lost control of that conversation with Reo so quickly? "Half a cup to finish off this awesome pie."

Lulu poured, her dour expression breaking into a slight grin. "Can't beat local strawberries and rhubarb. By the way, I support Allen's harvest theme, if you hadn't guessed." She cocked her head and narrowed her gaze. "Not sure what just went on between you and Reo, but don't think you can pull that stuff you pulled five years ago." She arched her brow at him.

"Yes, Ma'am." He never should've taken out his frustration by teasing Reo. But the mayor had really thrown him a curve in those moments before the meeting started.

"You don't want to help? Fine. Guess I'll have to tell Peacetalkers you ran into Reo Greene on purpose to settle an old score."

Whatever he'd been expecting the mayor to say in response to his refusal, it hadn't been that. All he needed was for someone to call Peacetalkers and tell them he was back in Lilac stirring up trouble by running into a girl who'd called the cops on him.

Oh yeah. That would go over just great right about now.

After settling his bill, he stepped outside into the midday sun and glanced around. Lilac was a far cry from the economically-depressed town he'd known as a kid. Gone were the crumbling curbs and outdated storefronts. Victorian park benches accented the sidewalks. Wrought iron street lamps highlighted quaint shop windows. During conversations at yesterday's 5K race, he'd learned the town's transformation was due in large part to the arrival of the solar plant. The upcoming anniversary celebration would be an opportunity to showcase the town's past and future. Was that why the mayor cared so much about the decoration proposals? He wanted to project the right image to promote future growth?

As he neared the Up Do salon, a well-dressed woman approached him with her hand outstretched.

"Jack, I'm so glad I ran into you."

He shook her hand. She'd been in that group of residents on Saturday. Another one of his mother's friends?

She must've seen his puzzled expression. "Kelly Prendergast. I gave you my real estate card at the race."

"Oh, right. Thank you." Hadn't there been a kid named Prendergast on the JV football team?

"The local housing market is booming right now thanks to the solar plant expansion." She pulled a brochure from her purse and stepped close enough for him to smell her flowery perfume. The overpowering scent nearly choked him. "Here's my contact information. Here are homes I've recently sold. I also provide free renovation advice. If there's anything you need, please don't hesitate to call." She slid the brochure into his hands, her fingers resting on his.

Was she flirting with him? He pushed away the thought, embarrassed. Small town folks were way more approachable than the city residents he'd grown accustomed to. Here people took time to stop and chat when others might hurry by. "Yes, ma'am, I'll keep that in mind."

"I'd be happy to come over and check out the property, give you an idea of its value."

"Sure, that'd be great." After she released his hand and moved on, he continued past the library and Filmore Hardware, making his way to Warfield's Garage. As he walked around the side of the building, his gaze traced the fire escape up to the dust-caked window on the second floor. His old apartment. His high school friends had christened it the Love Shack.

And they'd been madder than all get out when the

cops had shut him down.

He shoved his hands into his pockets, an uncomfortable twinge of guilt settling on him. It wasn't his fault if his friends had played tricks on Reo. Sure, he'd sat around, complaining about her, but he'd never told anyone to dump garbage in front of her locker. He stomped around the side of the building and plopped onto the worn wooden bench near the garage's rear entrance.

His uncle sat in a beaten-up lawn chair with his feet propped on an overturned bucket, reading glasses half way down his nose, flipping the pages of a car manual. "Aren't you worried about ruining your nice clothes?"

"Put 'em on just for you." Jack had spent a large part of his youth on this bench, shooting the breeze with the man who taught him the rules of small town life. Respect your elders. Do unto others. Mind the little things.

The corner of Pete's mouth twitched. "What did the mayor want?"

"Wants me and Reo to review the Main Street decoration proposals for the town's anniversary and make a recommendation."

Pete flipped a page. "Figured he'd punt when Lavinia submitted a proposal. Didn't think he'd kick it to you and Reo."

"He wants to make an example of us." Jack tugged at the collar of his shirt. Man, that sun was hot. "If we can get along for the good of the town, so can everybody else."

"An example." Pete chuckled as he took the pencil from behind his ear and scribbled a note in the margin. "So, he's guiltin' you into it."

"Arm twisting's more like it. He actually—" Wait a minute. Pete might just call the Peacetalkers himself if Jack told him what the mayor had threatened before Reo arrived. Pete would love it if the Peacetalkers fired him.

He sat back and crossed his arms. "You know, if you hadn't told me to stay away from Reo back in high school, none of this would've happened."

"So now you're blaming me for losing your scholarship?" Pete stared at Jack over the top of his reading glasses and shook his head.

"I'm not blaming anybody for anything." Jack shifted uncomfortably as old, unsettled feelings churned inside him. When his father had died, it was like a bomb had exploded inside him. He began running wild with his friends to prove he didn't care that the man whose opinion had meant so much was gone. His mother had gotten so fed up with his antics she'd made him move into the Warfield's Garage apartment when he'd turned eighteen.

And then that last party. He'd almost dropped dead with shock when Reo climbed through the window with that stream of kids. Driven by a sudden protective urge he'd never felt before, he'd grabbed Reo's hand and pulled her to the apartment's interior staircase, slamming the apartment door behind them. He'd hustled her down the dark steps, ignoring her protests, until they'd reached the bottom.

Then it happened. A shaft of moonlight through the open transom window transformed her face before his eyes. Radiant skin. Sapphire blue eyes. In that moment, she was the most beautiful girl he'd ever seen. He'd pulled her into his arms and kissed her, her mouth soft and yielding beneath his. When he'd come up for air, a cold wind through the transom slapped sense into him. Dragging his gaze from her parted lips, he'd shoved her outside and slammed the door.

He shook his head, remembering how good she'd felt in his arms. Blame? Might as well blame the moon.

Chapter Four

Reo stepped outside the DMV and winced. She had never been so ready for the end of her shift. What had she been thinking, wearing high heels to work? Her toes were swelled up like ten cherry tomatoes. She yanked off her sandals and walked barefoot down the sidewalk. She'd give anything right now for a pair of flip flops.

Lavinia Burgin stepped out of the bank in a swirl of leopard print, her pumps matching her dress. "Hey, Reo. Don't you look pretty?" She studied Reo's clothing. "I have silver earrings in my shop that would go perfectly with that necklace."

"Really?" Reo stepped on a pebble and flinched.

Lavinia focused her gaze downward and frowned. "What happened to your feet?"

"Wore the wrong shoes to work." Reo shifted back and forth as she lifted each foot in turn off the hot pavement.

Lavinia heaved a deep sigh, her gold medallion

sparkling in the late afternoon sun. "Yes, we women certainly have to suffer in the name of style. But beauty is a noble goal, don't you think?"

Except when her feet felt like pumpkins. "I guess so."

"I'm glad you agree." She brushed a lock of hair off her forehead. "I was a little worried when Tom told me you and Jack would be reviewing the Main Street decoration proposals."

Oh no, not now! Reo glanced around frantically. Sunny was just turning the Up Do Open sign to Closed. Reo reached for the handle and pushed open the door. "Good talking to you, Lavinia. Hey, Sunny."

Sunny glanced down. "What happened to your feet?"

"Stilettos." Reo shuddered.

Lavinia put her hand on Reo's shoulder. "Honey, a pedicure would do you a world of good. Some evenings, after standing behind the jewelry counter all day, I soak my feet for hours."

Sunny glanced down at her own sandal-clad feet and grinned. "Let's do it."

"Oh, Sunny," Lavinia said as Reo entered the shop. "I need to cancel my Wednesday appointment. Some of the town council members are taking a shopping trip to Charlottesville and won't be back in time. That reminds me. Reo, could you run the snack bar at The Lanes Wednesday evening?

Reo sighed. Her last exam was due Wednesday night. Still, snack bar profits went towards Lilac beautification. The town council needed to raise funds to continue replacing the old street lights with the beautiful wrought iron lamps that gave Main Street such a historic feel. She'd just have to make sure she finished and turned in her final exam early. Reo nodded. "Sure, I'll do it."

Lavinia pointed at Sunny. "You could help, too."

Sunny checked her phone. "I have a perm appointment that evening. If I can get my mom to take it, I'll be there."

"Wonderful. See you ladies later." Lavinia continued down the street to her shop.

Reo flipped on water jets and climbed into a pedicure chair. The warm swirling currents sent waves of relaxation through her entire body. Wednesday night at The Lanes. Better not forget. Too tired to even text herself a reminder, she sat back and closed her eyes.

"Let's order pizza." Sunny tapped her cell phone. "What did the mayor want with you and Jack?"

"He asked us to decide how to decorate Main Street for the two-hundred-fiftieth anniversary." She told Sunny about the mayor's predicament choosing a proposal and about Jack's background as a crisis mediator.

Sunny rolled a bottle of nail polish between her palms. "Jack's dreaming if he thinks this decoration thing can be settled quickly. My mom supports Lavinia's patriotic theme, my dad likes the harvest idea, and I want the lilacs."

"From his comments to me, it sounds like Jack wants to race through it so he can get back to D.C." Did he have a girlfriend?

"Speaking of racing, what if Jack did run into you on purpose at the 5K?"

"At first I thought that." Reo stared at the swirling water, her voice trailing off.

"What changed your mind?"

Reo pulled out her cell phone and handed it to Sunny.

Sunny stared at her phone a moment and then looked up. "What are those flapping wings?"

"It's an app I got in college. Jack has the same one on his phone."

"And this matters because?"

"Do you remember anything I told you about the semester I lived in the dorms?"

"Your one semester of misery." Sunny returned the phone. "Just that your mattress was lumpy, there was vomit in the hallway, and you hadn't made any friends as awesome as me."

"Pathetic and totally true." Reo lifted her feet out of the water and dried them. She reached for a bottle of pink nail polish and gave it a shake. "I did make one friend. She gave me this app when I helped her through a rough time."

Sunny filed her nails. "How does it work?"

"She touched her phone to mine and the app automatically appeared on my screen. It asked me to type my first name, then it assigned a number to me. I'm Reo12. She told me the app would make a fluttering sound whenever I was around people who'd helped someone and been given the app."

"So, Jack helped somebody who gave him the app." Sunny put her hands on her hips, her brown eyes flashing. "How come you never gave it to me? We've helped each other through lots of things."

Reo shifted uncomfortably. Why hadn't she given Sunny the app? "I guess once I got back I forgot about it. I've never given it to anyone."

Sunny's expression softened. "Kind of impossible to

feel alone in Lilac. I mean, look how much interest Lavinia took in your swollen feet."

"No kidding." Reo put the cap on the polish and set it aside while her nails dried. "Anyway, my phone and Jack's went off with this fluttering sound when we were at the scenic overlook."

Sunny's head jerked up. "You were at the scenic overlook with Jack?"

"I was at the scenic overlook with *Gina*. It was Mother's Day and—what?"

Sunny's hand flew to her mouth, her expression panicked. "Oh no! I meant to invite you over Sunday. Were you okay?"

"You mean did I burst into tears and totally embarrass myself like last year? No, thank goodness. Anyway, after Gina's boyfriend picked her up from the overlook, I was alone. The next thing I knew Jack was hiking up the trail and the app was going off on both our phones."

Sunny watched the little pair of silver wings flapping in the corner of Reo's phone. "Has it ever gone off for anyone else?"

Reo shook her head.

Sunny dabbed polish on her nails. "Well, Jack doesn't have to worry about being alone in Lilac."

"What do you mean?"

"Kelly Prendergast cornered him right in front of the shop window this afternoon. Slid up next to him, waving real estate brochures under his nose. Put on quite a show for the customers." Sunny sat back. "You should've heard their comments."

Reo bit her lip. She would not ask if Jack responded to Kelly's flirting. He could flirt with whomever he wanted. She walked over to the sink and washed her hands, then took off the necklace around her neck and handed it to Sunny. "Thanks for lending me this. Hey, I need to practice my interviewing skills. I thought maybe you and Miss Emma could help me."

"Sure." Sunny looked into the mirror. "You haven't said a word about my hair."

Reo smiled at Sunny's reflection. "I love the royal blue stripe. Think I could get away with that?"

Sunny shook her head. "Blue works best with dark hair like mine. You already have the perfect natural color. Do you know how many women come in here and want that exact shade of blonde? All I'd ever do with your hair is give it some layers. Show off your assets."

"Assets. Right."

Sunny studied her face. "Sure. Feather in some bangs to frame your eyes, accent the curve of your chin. Anytime you're ready for a change, let me know."

Change. Had Jack changed? After his attempt to have a little fun at The Shoebox this afternoon, she was inclined to think his wild streak was still in place, just camouflaged.

Reo's phone dinged.

9am tomorrow at the library?

Jack? Her phone didn't recognize the caller, but who else could it be? And how had he gotten her number? She tapped out her answer.

Ok but no fun.

Reo smiled to herself when he didn't reply.

~

Jack read the message a second time. *Ok but no fun.* What was that supposed to mean?

He looked around the barren kitchen, waiting, as if the faded walls of the house where he had grown up could speak and impart some wisdom. Not replying to Reo was certainly a negotiation tactic, although it wasn't clear exactly what he and Reo were negotiating at the moment. She'd agreed to meet him tomorrow morning. He'd leave it at that.

He shoved the phone into his jeans pocket and reached for a pair of pliers. Kneeling on discolored linoleum tile, he inspected the wiring where the old electric oven had been. Disconnecting the appliance and dragging it away from the wall had been the easy part. Dealing with the exposed mess of grease-coated drywall and rusted coils was another thing altogether.

Like coming back to Lilac. On the surface, the idea of returning home had sounded great. The leave of absence had left him with nothing to do in the city while he waited for the Peacetalkers to review what had happened. His mother needed to get her house on the market and he wanted to be busy. Figured he'd just cruise into his hometown, show everybody how he'd gotten his life together, and go back to his job in D.C.

Problem was, life wasn't that simple.

The Peacetalkers were launching a formal investigation.

Mayor Burgin had threatened to tell the Peacetalkers that Jack had intentionally run into Reo to settle an old score.

And then there was Reo herself. He sat back on his heels. He'd told her he was over losing the football scholarship. Was he? She certainly wasn't over the way he'd treated her at that party, or the way some of his friends had treated her afterwards.

What was that quote about God laughing when you tell Him your plans?

At the sound of boots stomping up the back porch steps he called over his shoulder, "Over here, Vejay." He'd been so relieved to see that Vejay Patel, one of his friends from high school, now owned an electrical contracting business. He'd called him as soon as he'd disconnected the oven.

"I'll tell him when he shows up," Pete answered as he walked through the screen door.

Jack stood at the sound of his uncle's voice and brushed the dust from his jeans.

Pete pointed at the corroded wire. "Finally met your match?"

"It's called delegation. Vejay is coming over to fix the wiring while I tackle the plumbing. What's that?" He watched as Pete pulled a card from his wallet and scribbled on the back.

"Plumber." Pete set the card on the counter.

"Thanks for the vote of confidence." The coffee maker gurgled. Jack walked over to the cabinet and took down two mugs. "Just made a fresh pot."

"No, thanks." Pete shoved his hands in his pocket. "What's this I hear about you getting into an argument with Reo at The Shoebox?"

The gossip mill didn't waste any time. Jack poured a cup of coffee and took a sip. "We were role playing. You know, making it look like we still hated each other but were going to work together for the good of the town."

"Role playing." Pete snorted. "Is that what you were doing with Kelly Prendergast in front of the Up Do?" His voice dripped with sarcasm.

Good to know the Lilac gossip mill was still in action. "I did not flirt with Kelly Prendergast. She was giving me real estate information."

"Well, don't think you can pull anything with Kelly. She could teach *you* a thing or two."

Jack crossed his arms. "Would that be based on firsthand knowledge?"

Pete glared at him.

Jack leaned against the counter. "Want me to call you when I set up an appointment with Kelly? I could arrange a surprise candlelight dinner for you two."

Pete's face turned three shades of red. He turned around and yanked open the screen door.

"Why'd you come over?" Jack called after him.

"Was gonna help, but I changed my mind." The door banged shut behind him.

Jack laughed as he watched Pete stomp down the porch steps. The Patel Electric van pulled into the driveway. Pete stood talking to Vejay for a moment, then climbed into his pickup and drove off.

Vejay carried a laptop into the kitchen and set it on the table. "Hey, man. How's it going?" Tall and lanky with jet black hair and dark eyes, Vejay hadn't changed a bit since high school.

Jack shook his hand. "I'll be doing a whole lot better when this house is on the market." And the stuff in D.C. is settled.

Vejay looked around, his gaze zeroing in on the exposed oven wires. He nodded. "Let's see what you've got."

After walking around the house for over an hour inspecting all the outlets, switches, and wiring, the two men settled at the kitchen table.

"Upgrade the kitchen wiring, install a new ceiling fan on the back porch," Vejay read from his list. "Replace the worn light switches and wall outlets. That's the minimum work that needs to be done to get this baby on the market."

Jack nodded. "Email me the estimate. I'll forward it to my mom. She's controlling the budget. I'm just overseeing the work."

"Nice of you to spend your vacation doing this for her."

Jack stared at the cracked linoleum as guilt pricked his conscience. He hadn't told anyone in Lilac about the leave of absence.

"How does it feel being back?" Vejay asked.

"Weird. Running into people I'd totally forgotten about. Seeing new businesses where old ones used to be. Say, I have a question for you."

"Shoot."

"Remember when Reo called the cops on my party?" Jack asked.

"Oh, my God, yes." Vejay laughed. "Sheriff Pettibone and our parents were waiting outside on the sidewalk. I got grounded for a month."

Jack nodded. "Everybody was really ticked with Reo afterwards."

"No kidding. One guy threw eggs at her car. Another kid doctored her senior picture to look like an old woman and posted it online." He shook his head. "I always felt bad she skipped prom because of that."

Ouch. He'd forgotten that. "Did you do anything?"

Vejay shook his head. "Already did something wrong by going to the party in the first place. Why would I get revenge on somebody who'd done the right thing?"

A sour feeling settled in Jack's stomach. "Do you remember me doing anything for revenge?"

Vejay gave him an odd look. "You're kidding."

Jack gripped his mug. "Just answer the question."

"You said something like she deserved to be annihilated, and if you weren't already in trouble, you'd do it yourself."

"I said that?"

"Yep. You were pretty drunk."

Had he really said that? Vague memories of gulping beers and stomping along the banks of Cool Water Run, ranting with his friends, filled his mind. "I was an idiot."

Vejay shrugged. "We were stupid teenagers. How's the new job?"

"Good." Jack shook off the troublesome memories and stood. "I was going to fire up the grill. You hungry?"

"Chaitra's waiting for me. We're eating with her parents tonight. Say, why don't you come bowling Wednesday night at The Lanes? Some team always needs a sub."

"You're kidding. You're in a league?" Bowling had always been a big deal in Lilac. Hard to believe guys he'd graduated high school with were now playing in the adult leagues.

Vejay grinned. "I bowl with The Casters, the Deutsch's Furniture team."

"Old man Deutsch still the captain?" Jack asked.

"Dewey's captain now. He's managing the store, too, now that his dad's retired."

Bowling? The last time he'd picked up a ball was in

some rec hall oversees. "You got shirts?"

"Of course." Vejay shook his hand. "I'll email the work estimate to you tomorrow."

As Jack watched Vejay's van pull away, his phone buzzed. A text from Steve.

Peacetalkers sent you a form to fill out.

He tapped the Peacetalkers email and opened the attachment. He scrolled through the form.

Please provide answers to the following questions regarding the incident. When did you arrange the meeting? Why didn't you notify Peacetalkers about it? Did you know the assailant?

A five-page questionnaire! They expected him to write a book about one little altercation?

The evening sun hung above the distant mountain range as the scent of lilacs drifted through the screen door. He leaned against the counter, watching until the golden orb dipped behind the ridge, then he shut the door and got to work.

Chapter Five

Reo walked through the library entrance at the stroke of nine Tuesday morning, her backpack heavy on her shoulders. She came to an abrupt stop. Jack stood with Miss Emma in front of the library's Welcome Center display, gaze fixed on something hanging on the wall, his expression serious. Dressed in faded jeans and a black tee shirt, he'd ditched the professional persona he'd projected yesterday for the meeting with the mayor. She smoothed her hair into place and strolled towards them. "What's everybody so—oh!"

Jack glanced at her, his gaze somber.

Reo studied the display. *Memorial Day: Remembering Lilac's Heroes.* Vintage photographs of the town's veterans, men and women in uniform who'd proudly served and lost their lives, hung in the display area. Her gaze followed Jack's to the picture of his father, a young and handsome Sean Warfield, standing at attention in his uniform.

"I was just telling Jack a story about when his father

was a student. I could always count on Sean to ask a question about some faraway place I'd never heard of." Miss Emma smiled. "So curious and eager to travel."

"Well, he certainly got his wish when he joined the army." Jack folded his arms across his chest and shifted his weight to his back foot.

"Where were some of the places he went?" Reo asked, the huskiness of her voice surprising her. She cleared her throat.

"He never told me. He was a Ranger. Couldn't talk about his work." Jack shoved his hands into his pockets.

Miss Emma pointed at another photograph. "Paul here was a Ranger as well. And Clayton was a Navy Seal." She wagged her finger at the display. "I'd have a lot more pictures to show if Harlan Howell would give me access to *The Sentinel* archives. When I think of all those photos sitting in his attic, it's all I can do not to put a ladder against his house and climb up."

"Why won't Harlan let you use the newspaper archives?" Jack asked, his tone curious.

Reo smiled, grateful for Miss Emma's ability to transform the serious atmosphere with her feistiness.

Miss Emma folded the flaps of her cardigan across her chest. "He claims the last time he lent me photos, they came back damaged."

"Were they?" Jack asked.

Miss Emma's shoulders slumped. "Thumb tack holes at the corners. One of my eager volunteers thought she'd surprise me and decorate the bulletin board while I was gone. I never had the chance to tell her the images needed to be put inside protective plastic sheets which could then be hung without damaging the photos."

Reo slid her arm around Miss Emma's shoulders. "Harlan's usually pretty reasonable. Did you explain what happened?"

Miss Emma shook her head. "I've called, sent him a letter, even knocked on his door, but he won't respond. I saw him a few days ago in Filmore Hardware and he dodged away faster than a scalded dog. He bought the town's history when he bought *The Sentinel* newspaper archives. I don't know what I'll do for the town's anniversary celebration if he doesn't change his mind. I promised the town council I'd have a different display each month, highlighting Lilac's history."

The bell on the circulation desk sounded. As Miss Emma headed off to help a customer, Reo led the way to a table in the back next to the window.

Jack gave her a curious look. "This was my table."

She snorted. "Right. The two times you were here. This was my table." She pointed out the window. "Direct view of the Up Do. I could wave to Sunny while she was helping her mom."

He reached under the table like he was looking for something. "I may not have come here as often as you, but I have proof. Look."

She bent down and looked under the table. "What?"

"Here." He took her hand and guided it to a spot on the rough underside. His skin warmed hers as he gently pressed her fingers against the wood. "Feel that?"

J.W. Heat spread up her arm. "Vandal."

His dark eyes gazed into hers at much too close a range. After a moment, he cleared his throat and released her hand. "Let's walk along Main Street, try to imagine what each person is proposing. What's all that?" He nodded at her backpack.

"Homework. I have two online exams due tomorrow."

"You're still in school?" He looked shocked. "Thought you'd have graduated by now."

He didn't have to look so stunned. "I'll get my diploma in August."

"What's your major?"

"Education," she said with a smile.

He rolled his eyes. "Teacher. Why am I not surprised?"

"What do you have against school? Wait, forget I asked that." She stored her backpack at the circulation desk with Miss Emma for safekeeping and followed Jack outside.

"Ignore cost for a minute." He slipped on his sunglasses as they descended the library steps. "Let's explore all the options. Try to envision how each of the proposals would be implemented. How would Mrs. Newmacher decorate with lilacs?"

She slipped on her own sunglasses, impressed. Maybe he really was going to take this assignment seriously. She scanned the proposals as they walked along Main Street. "Mrs. Newmacher says she'd fill all existing flower boxes, planters, and hanging baskets with purple, pink, white, and blue lilacs. She'd also place vases of fresh lilacs in every shop window." She glanced around and tried to imagine the vivid blossoms she'd seen lining the road to the scenic overlook transported here to Main Street. "I think it would be beautiful."

He looked up and down the block, his expression thoughtful. "How frequently would they have to be watered? How often would she have to replace them?

I'm no expert, but cut flowers don't last long. She'd probably need a team of people to gather the dying blossoms and replace them."

She flipped through the pages. "She doesn't say anything about watering, how long they'd last, or how frequently they'd have to be replaced."

He pulled out a pen and scribbled on the back of his proposal. "The mayor didn't say anything about follow-up questions, but I think we may need to ask some."

"I agree." She paused at the Up Do's front window and waved to Sunny. All the women inside the salon stared as Jack slipped his arm around Reo's shoulders and waved back. Sunny wagged a finger at them and mouthed *I told you so.*

"What are you doing?" Reo asked, her lips freezing in a smile despite the warmth his arm around her was generating.

He waved to their audience. "Yesterday people saw us arguing in The Shoebox. Today we're working together. That should make the mayor happy."

She shot him a look. "I thought I told you no fun."

"You think this is fun? Just feeding the gossip mill." He lowered his arm and resumed walking.

What was going on? Yesterday he'd sounded like he couldn't wait to get this assignment over with. Today, he was worried about creating a good impression. She glanced at his profile, confused.

He stopped walking suddenly, his expression serious. "I owe you an apology for turning my friends against you after that party. No wonder you thought I ran into you on purpose. I'd forgotten the things I'd said, but Vejay reminded me how angry I'd been. I personally didn't pull any pranks on you, but I might as well have." He shoved his hands in his pockets. "I'm sorry."

She studied his serious expression. "Wow, you took my no fun comment literally."

His brows shot up. "Are you always this direct?"

"Only with my sworn enemies and from what I heard, you did a lot of swearing after the cops came." She narrowed her gaze. "You know, this could be interesting. You as the serious one and me making the jokes."

The scent of fresh basil tickled her nose. She turned towards the entrance of Allen and Eva's Organic Produce.

Jack put his hand against the produce display table, blocking her path. "Forgetting something?"

She bumped into his arm. "What?" she asked, wishing she weren't so aware of his touch.

He cocked his brow. "Aren't you going to apologize for calling the cops?"

She stepped back, grateful for the sunglasses shielding her eyes from his scrutiny. "No. I was right."

"Uh-huh. Those parties had been going on for weeks. You could've called the cops any time." He leaned close. "Did you call because I threw you out or because I kissed you?"

"Because you broke the law." She ducked under his arm and scurried to the entrance. The store chimes jingled as she hurried into Allen and Eva's Organic Produce. They almost drowned out the sound of Jack's laughter as he followed her inside.

~

The aroma of fresh spices—cinnamon, oregano, pepper—filled the air. Shelves made of unfinished planks held wicker baskets filled with beats, onions, and bell peppers. Thick wood beams crossed a bright white ceiling. Pots of fresh herbs sat on top of hay bales. Canning books and supplies lined the wall across from quart boxes of fresh strawberries.

Jack felt like he'd stepped back in time to some rustic country market. His mouth watered at the smell of roasting peanuts. "Didn't this used to be a shoe store?"

"The shoe store closed right after you left," Reo said over her shoulder. She introduced him to Allen Owens, and the two men shook hands.

Dressed in a plaid shirt and worn overalls with the shop's logo printed on the bib, Allen looked like a man completely in his element and happy to be there. "My wife, Eva, runs the farm, I sell the produce," Allen explained as they stood at the front counter.

"Did you grow all this?" Jack gestured to the colorful array of fruits and vegetables.

"Just the local produce. Things that aren't in season right now, like blueberries, cantaloupes, and cucumbers, I get from my cousin in Florida. Later on, I'll ship him fruits he can't grow down there like apples and peaches."

Jack nodded. "Impressive."

"So, you two are reviewing the anniversary decoration proposals." He eyed Jack and Reo, his gaze speculative. "Back in the day, folks depended on this region's abundant produce to survive. That's why I think we ought to commemorate the harvest for the town's anniversary celebration."

"Are you planning on using fresh produce or pictures of fresh produce in your displays?" Jack asked.

"Both. Look at this." Allen retrieved a flyer from behind the counter and held it up. "Allen and Eva's Organic Produce is sponsoring a high school art contest. We're asking students to draw pictures of local fruit and vegetables that can be hung as part of the anniversary celebration."

Jack flipped through the proposal pages. "That wasn't part of your original plan."

Allen beamed. "Nope. Just thought of it last night."

Reo's face broke into a huge smile. "What a great idea."

"Figured you'd like it, seeing as how you want to be a high school teacher." Allen winked.

Jack's gaze flew to Reo's face, watching as her cheeks turned pink.

A buzzing sound came from the back of the store. Allen set the flyer on the counter. "That's the delivery truck. Let me know if you have any questions about my proposal."

After Allen disappeared down the aisle, Jack leaned against the counter. "Are you going to teach at Lilac Mountain High?"

"I hope to. I submitted my application." Reo's face turned bright red. "You think Allen suggested the art contest when he learned the mayor had asked us to review the proposals?"

"I think he suggested the art contest when he learned the mayor had asked *you*."

Reo's eyes widened. Without a word, she spun around and left the store.

What the heck? She was almost halfway down the block before Jack caught up with her. "Where are you going? We're not done yet."

She continued to hurry, eyes fixed front. "It's later than I thought. I have schoolwork I need to finish. Can't we continue this tomorrow?" The words spilled rapidly from her lips.

One minute they were talking, the next minute she was running away. He touched her arm. "Did I say something to upset you?"

She slowed her steps. "I'm really worried about these take-home exams. I need to do a good job on them."

Why wouldn't she look at him? They approached the library steps. Jack cast a glance at the entrance. "Is it still Catfish Tuesday at the Yacht Club?"

That stopped her. "Far as I know."

"And you have to take a break from your schoolwork to eat dinner?" He held his breath, waiting, until she nodded. "Then how about we kill three birds with one stone? Eat catfish, continue discussing the proposals, and ambush Harlan Howell."

She spun around. "What?"

"You heard me. We should find out why Harlan is being a jerk about refusing to share the archives with Miss Emma."

She crossed her arms. "Jerk. Is that a formal negotiation term?"

"No. That would be intransigent party."

She cocked her head, her expression skeptical. "I thought you wanted to finish this task as soon as possible."

"I do. But I also want to help Miss Emma. Those pin holes were not her fault."

"Why do you care?"

"Miss Emma stood up for me when nobody else

did." It felt strange to admit that. He'd carried that gratitude inside him all these years and never voiced it.

Reo's glance moved to the library entrance, her expression wary. "Miss Emma speaks her mind and some people don't like it. I'm not sure we should get involved."

"Look, the mayor asked us to make recommendations regarding the town's decorations. Far as I'm concerned, Miss Emma's proposal to decorate the library is related to that." Jack watched the hesitation play across her face.

"Maybe one conversation," she said finally. "Just to find out why."

~

Jack recalled Reo's reluctance later that evening as he followed the five-mile trail through the woods to the Yacht Club. He inhaled the loamy air as the path wound along the river. Asking her to meet at the hole in the wall had been a Hail Mary play. As soon as the words were out of his mouth, he'd worried Reo would be insulted by his suggestion. The Yacht Club was a tumble-down shack where folks feasted on whatever local fishermen caught in the river, fried up by the proprietor Wiley Abernathy and spiced so hot it could make a nose run for a week. And when the fish weren't biting, the customers dined on homemade beef jerky and whatever fresh kill some hunter brought in for dressing.

But she'd agreed. Either Reo really liked catfish or she really wanted to help Miss Emma. And everybody knew Harlan Howell had been eating catfish there on Tuesdays for decades. If they wanted to talk to Harlan in an informal, non-confrontational atmosphere, the

Yacht Club was the place to do it.

The crickets chirped along with the groaning tree frogs as the night creatures came to life. Jack swatted the mosquitos attacking his neck. Couldn't these critters smell bug repellant? He'd headed into the woods right before sunset, eager to walk the old trails he'd explored as a kid. Now as he followed the path overlooking Cool Water Run, he watched the last vestiges of reflected sunlight disappear from the river's surface. How many hours had he spent on the banks of this river, planning his escape from Lilac? Of course, back then, he'd had dreams of being a star fullback, not a soldier, and certainly not a crisis negotiator.

Would that dream be taken away from him, too? Earlier in the day he'd glanced again at the Peacetalkers' questions regarding his injury and quickly closed the email. He had plenty of time to send them his answers.

The cries of geese high overhead reverberated through the cool mountain air. He flipped on the flashlight and continued down the trail, picking up his pace as the path turned away from the river and headed up the bank. What was that light over the rise? He climbed to the top and halted at the edge of the forest. What the heck? A well-dressed, middle-aged couple emerged from an expensive sedan parked in a brightly lit parking lot filled with cars. Arm-in-arm, they strolled into what appeared to be a newly built rustic-style inn, complete with red painted shutters and candles in the windows.

Son of a gun! In the old days, a person could only get to the Yacht Club by boat or by foot or with a truck built for off-roading. No wonder Reo had given him that funny look when he'd invited her to hike the five miles with him. *I'll meet you there*, she'd said with a grin.

Reeking of insect repellant, he glanced down at his muddy boots, torn jeans, and faded plaid shirt. He strode across the parking lot and around the fancy restaurant building. Squatting in the shadows a couple dozen yards from the new restaurant was the original weather-beaten Yacht Club, slanted roof and rickety steps intact. The hum of country music punctuated by boisterous laughter floated through the screened windows.

He pulled open the creaking door and stepped inside. This was more like it. Air heavy with sweat and the grease of frying catfish swirled beneath vintage ceiling fans. His gaze adjusted to the dim interior and his mouth dropped open. Women and men stood talking and laughing at the counter where folks used to gut fish. Couples Texas Two-Stepped across a corner dance floor. Like Lilac's Main Street, the place had lost some of its rough edges.

He pushed through the crowd. Some of these folks had milled around him the morning of the 5K race, but darn if he could remember anybody's name. Then he saw her. At the far end of the counter, wearing a short white skirt that showed off her long, tanned legs, Reo stood with her shoulder pressed against some guy's arm. Jack froze, his gaze riveted on the two figures huddled together.

Did she have a boyfriend?

As if sensing Jack's intense gaze, the guy turned around, his red hair curling around his ears. "Warfield?"

Jack took a step back. "Dewey?" With his wavy red hair and paunch, Dewey Deutsch was the spitting image of his father. Jack's face relaxed into a smile of relief as he shook Dewey's hand.

Dewey grinned. "Heard you were back. Reo was just telling me how the mayor snagged you to review the Main Street decoration proposals."

Reo inclined her head toward Dewey's phone. "He likes Lavinia's theme."

Jack looked at the picture of Deutsch's Furniture store decorated with red-white-and-blue streamers.

"We can use the Fourth of July decorations we already have," Dewey explained. "No use buying anything new. I don't want people putting baskets of pumpkins and tomatoes on my polished tables. And depending on the exact shade of lilac, the blossoms could clash with the upholstery."

Exact shade of lilac? Jack bit the inside of his lip. Never thought he'd hear the high school class clown discussing colors schemes. Dewey must've grown into his role as heir apparent of Deutsch's Furniture. "Makes sense."

Reo gave Jack a pointed look. "You missed Harlan. He was walking out the door just as I was walking in."

"What do you need to see Harlan for?" Dewey asked.

Jack explained Harlan's refusal to lend the newspaper archives to the library for the celebration.

Dewey looked confused. "Why does that matter to you?"

"Harlan is denying the library access to the archives because of a few accidental pin holes. Way too harsh."

"Jack's a crisis negotiator," Reo said with a grin.

"He thinks he can change Harlan's mind."

"Good luck with that. When you're done, see if you can get him to modify the rules for the bowling league Mystery Game."

"Mystery Game?" Jack asked, bewildered.

Reo rested her hand on Jack's forearm, her gaze bright. "Where scores from randomly picked games are added together, and the bowler with the highest score wins. Come on, you remember."

His heart kicked up a notch. Darn if he could remember anything with her holding his arm and staring at him like that. "Maybe."

"Some of the teams want the Mystery Game rules changed," Dewey explained. "But Harlan won't budge."

Reo pursed her lips. "Sounds intransigent."

Jack swallowed a smile. "Vejay asked me to come by The Lanes tomorrow night and be a sub. Will Harlan be there? What?"

Reo was giving him the funniest look. "Lavinia asked me to volunteer at The Lanes' snack bar tomorrow night." She leaned back against the counter and grinned. "Can't wait to see the master negotiator in action."

Jack held her gaze, accepting the challenge he heard in her voice. "You're in for a thrill."

Dewey looked back and forth between them. "I thought you two hated each other."

Reo brushed her hair off her shoulders. "We do. This is all an act we're putting on to help the mayor, right Jack?" She cocked her brow at him.

Her playful challenge kicked his pulse up another notch. "Hey, aren't we supposed to be eating catfish?"

He shook Dewey's hand. "Tomorrow, man."

Turning, he reached for Reo's hand and led her through the crowd to an empty table near the dance floor. Lifting his arm, he gave her a spin in time to the music.

She floated into her chair with the grace of a ballerina. "What are you doing?" Her voice had a breathless quality he'd never heard before.

"Just keeping my word to the mayor." He said, wondering suddenly what he'd have to do to hear that breathless voice again.

Chapter Six

Reo watched the dancers move in the familiar Texas Two-Step pattern. Step together-walk-walk. Step together-walk-walk. Maybe if she kept watching them she wouldn't have to acknowledge the curious looks she and Jack were getting from the patrons. Many of them were all too familiar with the blistering history she and Jack shared.

Her gaze rested on Jack's open collar, the triangle of tanned skin it revealed. After that spontaneous little twirl, no one would believe they were enemies now. She was starting to have a difficult time believing it herself.

Her gaze moved across the packed dance floor and crowded tables, taking in the faces of friends who came here to eat and socialize. The smell of catfish permeated the air, making her mouth water. She couldn't remember the last time she'd been here. Sunny's twenty-first birthday? Maybe that fundraiser for the high school band? She pulled out her phone to check for an email from the high school. They had to be contacting her about an interview soon.

Jack studied her from across the table. "Weird, huh?"

She nodded and put away her phone. "Yeah, who would've thought you could pull off a dance move like that."

He shook his head, his expression serious. "You do that a lot."

"What?"

He threw his arm over the back of his chair. "Make jokes when someone is trying to have a serious conversation. Either that or you run away like you did this afternoon."

She squirmed, inching her chair away from the table. "What are you talking about?"

He lifted his hand, two fingers raised, and nodded at the waitress across the room. "Today. One minute we were talking about Allen's proposal. The next minute you were running to the library."

She shook her hair off her shoulders. "I had exams to finish and turn in."

"Did you get them finished?" A lock of hair fell across his forehead as he cocked his head.

"Yes." She'd submitted the online exams just before leaving for the Yacht Club. She'd have gotten them done sooner if she hadn't been so distracted thinking about their morning together.

"Congratulations." He pinned her with a serious gaze. "Still say you were running away."

She lifted her chin. "You implied Allen was trying to bribe me."

He leaned forward. "I didn't say you were going to

take it.”

“I don’t know how to take you.”

“What’s that supposed to mean?”

No one else spoke to her the way he did. Challenging her. Questioning her behavior. She flattened her palms on the table. “One minute you’re colliding with me in the street, the next minute you’re spinning me to my seat. I don’t know what you’re up to.” She threw her hands in the air.

His expression sobered. He blew out a long breath. “I wouldn’t be up to anything if the mayor weren’t twisting my arm.”

Her hands froze. “What?”

He was silent as the waitress brought their food. Two plates of steaming catfish, homemade coleslaw, and fresh cornbread. He glanced around as if to see who was in hearing distance. “I was involved in a negotiation that went sour and resulted in injuries. When that happens, the group I work for, the Peacetalkers, investigates.”

Peacetalkers? She felt the anger drain out of her, replaced by surprise. Whatever she’d been expecting, it hadn’t been that.

He took a sip of water. “The mayor said if I didn’t help evaluate the decoration proposals, he’d tell the Peacetalkers I ran into you on purpose to settle an old score.”

She picked up her fork and poked the flaky, perfectly cooked fish. “Did you?”

“No,” he answered, his tone sincere. “When I saw that stupid banner, I lost my footing and stumbled.”

She reached for a piece of the cornbread and set it down. The country music slowed to three-four waltz time as the dancers swirled past. "Would you really lose your job if Mayor Burgin told them?"

"I might."

"Were you hurt?"

"Knife wound. Couple stitches. Both my mom and Pete want me to quit." He forked up a bite of fish.

She would, too. When Mayor Burgin announced that Jack was a mediator, it never occurred to her that there could be violence involved. "What exactly does a mediator do?"

"Try to help people reach agreements. People who can't stand each other. People who want to kill each other."

"What kind of agreements?"

"Like getting drug dealers to stay out of soup kitchens."

How could he say that so matter-of-factly? She set down her fork, her appetite gone. "You're kidding."

He continued eating. "Turf battles. Recruiting teenagers."

She leaned back. Jack sat before her calmly eating, dressed in a flannel shirt and jeans. Anyone looking would think he was one of the locals just come in from a lazy day fishing on the river. Nobody would think he was risking his life, trying to help others.

He set down his fork. "You'll be dealing with some of these things as a high school teacher. Maybe not on the same scale. Peacetalkers send speakers into schools to help with gang violence, bullying, drug use. Maybe here in Lilac those aren't big issues. But twenty miles up the road these problems occur in economically depressed rural towns just like they do in cities."

She nibbled her lip. Was that one of the reasons Gina

had lost interest in her studies? Carsondale hadn't bounced back economically like Lilac had, didn't have the solar plant or the active town council that focused on renovations and town improvements. When the state government had been trying to decide what town to put the new DMV satellite office in, they'd picked Lilac over Carsondale. One more reason Lilac was thriving.

Jack's glance moved over her shoulder. His face broke into a big smile. "Hey, isn't that Donnie?"

She turned around, her fork halfway to her mouth. Dad? Who was he dancing with? Oh my God. She looked back down at her food. "I'm not hungry anymore. Ready to go?"

Jack glanced at her half-eaten fish. "You've hardly touched your food."

She angled her chair so she was no longer facing the dance floor. "I want to go. Stay if you want. I'm leaving." She reached for her purse, her heart suddenly racing.

His hand circled her wrist. "The woman Donnie's dancing with. Who is she?" he asked calmly.

Why did he have to be so observant? Her pulse pounded in her ears. She leaned across the table. "My boss," she hissed.

Jack's eyebrows raised then settled back into place. He released her wrist and took a long time dabbing his mouth with his napkin.

She slammed her napkin onto the table. He was laughing at her.

"Running again? I take it this is a surprise." He pulled out his wallet and tossed some bills on the table. "You've got two choices. Slink around the walls toward the exit and hope Donnie doesn't see, although everyone else will. Or walk over, say good evening, and leave through the front entrance with a big wave for the crowd. Which one is it?"

She slid her chair away from the table. "You can do whatever you want. I'm using the back door." When Donnie and Leanne reached the far end of the dance floor, she jumped to her feet and dashed into the kitchen.

"Hey, Wiley. Delicious, as always," she called out as she squeezed between the cluttered counter and Wiley Abernathy's massive frame, careful not to get too close to the sizzling deep fryer. She hurried down the back steps and around the building to the parking lot. She saw her father's car beneath a streetlamp and Leanne's little blue hybrid right next to it. Were they dating? How long had they kept this a secret from her? She fished inside her purse, looking for her keys as she approached her car. Footsteps pounded behind her. She turned around.

Donnie faced her, dressed in his white country-and-western shirt with the blue embroidery, his best jeans, and cowboy boots. The streetlight illuminated the silver streaks in his hair. "Reo?"

Her gaze shot to Leanne and Jack, standing a few steps behind him. Awkward. "Hey, Dad. How's it going?"

Donnie stepped closer, spread his hands. "Jack said you left when you saw Leanne and me dancing." He rubbed the back of his neck. "Guess I should've told you we were going out. Tried to the other morning. You've been so busy with the 5K race and your schoolwork."

"That's okay, Dad. Really. It's fine if you and

Leanne are going out." She waved to Leanne and forced her lips so wide they hurt. "Hey, Leanne. Really, it's fine." Could her voice sound any more fake?

Donnie shoved his hands in his pockets. "This is our first date. We had a great time Friday night at the Moose Lodge Texas Two-Step contest. Came in second place. Decided to meet here tonight to get more practice."

"That's great, Dad. Honest, I'm glad." She glanced at Leanne. "Just surprised."

Leanne stepped forward to stand next to Donnie. "I wanted to tell you, too. I hope things will be okay at work."

Reo's head shook like a bobble-head doll. "Of course. They'll be fine." Please let them just go away.

Donnie jerked a thumb over his shoulder. "You want to come back inside with us? I bet Jack knows a few more dance moves." He winked at her.

So, Dad had seen Jack spin her into her seat. Reo gripped the handle of her purse. "No, thanks. I have some schoolwork to finish up." Which wasn't exactly a lie. She'd turned in both of her exams earlier, but still had teacher evaluations to complete.

Donnie leaned forward and kissed her cheek. "See you at home then."

Reo watched as Donnie and Leanne walked across the parking lot, their heads together, talking. After they turned the corner, she shook her finger at Jack. "You had no right to do that."

Jack sauntered to her side. "That's what most of my clients say when I bring them together."

"So, I'm your client now?" She yanked open the car door and climbed inside. Where were her keys? She rooted through her purse, refusing to look at Jack.

"In exchange for ignoring your infantile behavior, how about you give me a ride home." It wasn't a question. He strode to the passenger door and yanked it open.

She shoved the keys into the ignition and started the engine. "I don't know what you're so upset about. It was *my* dad dancing with *my* boss." She stepped on the gas and pulled out of the lot.

Jack rolled down his window, letting the cool air rush in.

She drove in silence, focusing on the dark road illuminated only by her headlights. The winding trail wove down the hill and along the ridge overlooking the river. Moonlight sparkled on the still water.

"Doesn't Donnie go on dates?" Jack asked. "I don't see what the big deal is."

She tapped her finger against the wheel. "I'll tell you what the big deal is. Leanne is my boss. They should have told me."

"Because?"

Was he dense? "She's my boss. What's there not to get? No matter what Leanne says, it's going to be awkward."

"Still not getting it. You want to be a teacher in this town. There will be parents confronting you at The Shoebox because you gave their kids an F. How are you gonna deal with that?"

Hands tight on the wheel, she turned off the gravel road onto the street leading into town. "Just because you went off and became a big hero doesn't give you the right to preach at me."

"I'm not preaching. This is dialogue. Two people

with a difference of opinion discussing it. We both have valid points."

She turned onto Main Street. "There's right and there's wrong and there's consequences. You were trying to negotiate, somebody got violent, now you're on leave of absence. Right, wrong, consequence. My dad dating is fine. My dad dating my boss is not fine. Leanne's going to start acting weird, and that's a consequence I do not want to deal with." She pulled up in front of his house. She could feel Jack's gaze burning her profile.

"You talk just like a school teacher." He climbed out of the car and slammed the door.

"That's the goal," she shouted through the open window. She threw the car into gear and sped away. Who did he think he was? Heart pounding, she drove a few blocks to her own driveway. To think she once daydreamed about Jack returning to Lilac. For all she knew, he was lying about the mayor twisting his arm just to make her feel sorry for him.

Hurrying up the porch steps, she stomped into her bedroom and slammed the door. Her phone buzzed. Silver wings filled her screen, this time above a message:

Jack3387: Time to put away childish things.

Was Jack using that app to lecture her? She threw her cell phone on the bed. She could not work with him. Tomorrow she would tell Mayor Burgin the deal was off.

~

On Wednesday morning at ten, Jack settled into the worn leather armchair facing Harlan Howell's desk. He couldn't believe his luck. Harlan had taken his early morning call and agreed to see Jack in his office. Make that man cave. Dark-paneled walls surrounded the imposing, white-haired man seated behind the massive desk. Green-shaded lamps cast dim beams of light on worn oriental carpets and faded draperies. No way to tell from the gloomy interior that outside it was bright and sunny.

After the way he and Reo had parted the night before, there was no way he was going to have a negotiation with Harlan tonight at a crowded bowling alley in front of her. He'd negotiate here by candle light if he had to.

Harlan puffed on his cigar and leaned back in his chair, twisting his mouth to angle a stream of smoke toward the ceiling. "I hear you're fixing up your momma's house to sell."

"Yes, sir, that's the idea." Jack shifted in his chair, the cracked leather poking his back. Had he gone too far, sending Reo that message through the app? Couldn't she see she was acting like a kid?

Harlan tapped his cigar in the ash tray. "And you want my advice."

Jack nodded towards the state map hanging on the wall beside Harlan's desk. "From what I hear, you know more about real estate than anyone in Lilac."

"Anyone in Hamilton County," Harlan corrected.

Jack inclined his head. The air reeked of stale smoke. Did the man ever open a window? The side wall was covered with framed licenses and diplomas. CPA. Law Degree. Real Estate license. Notary public. Harlan was a one-man financial services company. Totally old school. "I suppose you heard the mayor asked me and Reo Greene to evaluate the decoration proposals for the two-hundred-fiftieth anniversary celebration."

Harlan's chair squeaked as he leaned forward, resting his forearms on the blotter with a scowl. "Folks in this town are blind. Arguing over what color pansies to plant on Main Street when there are much bigger fish to fry."

"Like what?"

"Like an assisted living facility for the senior citizens of this town. Do you know how big that segment of our population has become? I've been working for over a year trying to get that deal negotiated. Got land picked out. Got a builder who wants to come in and develop it. But Tom Burgin's throwing up roadblocks."

Interesting. Jack leaned back in his chair. "What kind of roadblocks?"

"The invisible kind. Pride. Arrogance. Jealousy that he didn't think of it first. That solar plant's only a few years old, but in another decade, there will be employees who want to retire. Do we want them moving to Florida or out West? No sirree Bob. We want them to stay right here in Lilac in a modern facility with all the amenities. Encourage their families who come to visit to stay and settle. Keep Lilac growing."

He had to hand it to the old guy. It made sense. "You got the plans?"

Harlan shuffled to his corner cabinet, reached in, and pulled out a big cardboard tube. He extracted the rolled up architectural plans and spread them on the desk. "Sure do. Look at this."

Jack stood and studied the drawings. Why would the mayor block an assisted living facility? "Maybe I can help."

Harlan cocked his brow at him. "That so?"

Jack flipped through the charts. "The mayor owes me. But I'm going to need something from you."

Harlan stared him down, his blue eyes narrowing to two laser points. After a moment, he let out a hoot and slapped his blotter. "Haven't had a good negotiation since I bought the rights to *The Sentinel* newspaper archives. What are you after, son?"

Jack leaned forward and rested his hands on the desk. "Access to the newspaper archives."

Harlan's jaw dropped. "What do you need that for?"

"Not for me. For the library."

Harlan stiffened. "Don't go sticking your nose where it don't belong."

"Look, I owe Miss Emma. She didn't damage those photographs. A well-intentioned volunteer did. You're a lawyer. The punishment doesn't fit the crime."

Harlan sank into his chair, a brooding expression settling onto his wrinkled features. He scowled. "When *The Sentinel* went belly up, I used my own money to purchase those archives. Town council wouldn't spend a nickel to save them. Those archives contain the entire history of Lilac. Can't have people who don't know what they're doing handling one-of-a-kind documents and photographs."

Jack sat. "But hoarding them in your house is not helping to tell the town's story. There's got to be a way to share them."

Harlan drummed his fingers on the desktop. "I don't have the time or the knees to be running up to the attic and hunting for information every time Emma Farquar wants to hang a new display."

"Then move the archives to the library."

Harlan chomped on his cigar. "Out of the question."

"The material could be scanned and put online. Volunteers could be trained on how to handle it correctly. I bet the county historical society could send somebody over to talk about proper storage and preservation."

"You just listed a bunch of conditions I would require before I let anyone touch those files."

Jack reached for a blank tablet of paper and a pen. "Then let's finish the list."

Harlan's pale blue eyes couldn't have popped open any wider if he'd been hit by a thunderbolt. "You got the knack for deal-making, I'll give you that." He chuckled. "Tell me something. Are you really selling your momma's house?"

"Yes, sir."

"And you really need advice?"

Jack focused on the list. "More than you know."

"You owe Miss Emma and the mayor owes you." Harlan puffed on his cigar. "If you can pull off these deals, I'll owe you, too."

~

On Wednesday morning, Reo approached the DMV's employee entrance and took a deep breath to steady her nerves. Her dad was dating her boss. She could deal with it. She had to.

The words of Jack's message had replayed in her mind last night as she'd tried to sleep, fueling her agitation. Her tossing and turning was finally interrupted by the sound of whistling—her father's whistling—drifting through her bedroom window as he came home from his date.

Tears had filled her eyes. When was the last time she'd heard her father whistle? Or seen him dance? If he was happy with Leanne, what right did she have to get upset about it? She'd be quitting her job at the DMV when she started teaching at Lilac Mountain High.

Forgive me, God, for being so selfish.

Her dad deserved to be happy. She hated admitting Jack may have been right. But just because he was right about Dad and Leanne didn't mean she had to work with him. Jack made her feel self-conscious, like she had to question everything she did. She'd tell Mayor Burgin that Jack was more than capable of evaluating the proposals without her.

She pushed open the DMV entrance and walked in. A group of older men from the road crew sat sipping coffee by the vending machines.

"Whoa, Reo!"

"Looking good, kid."

"Who are you trying to impress?"

Reo rolled her eyes at the chorus of male voices. "What is this? High school?" She reached for her timecard and punched in. "Can't a person get dressed up for work?"

"Looks just like Carly Day," someone muttered behind her back.

Another voice whispered in response. The men chuckled.

Heat flooded her face as she walked down the hall to the employee lockers, the skirt of her flowery blue dress slapping against her legs. She was not like Carly Day. She pushed the locker shut.

"Good morning, Reo." Leanne stood at the far end of

the room, her hand gripping the doorframe as if she couldn't decide whether to come in or stay out.

Reo took a deep breath. She could do this. She looked up and smiled. "Morning, Leanne."

Leanne's gaze took in her dress. "You look nice."

"Thanks." How long could she hold this smile?

Leanne stared at her a moment longer as if she couldn't figure out what to say next. "Thank you for being early."

"No problem." Awkward.

"Guess we better get to work. Mid-week rush." She hurried past Reo to the lobby entrance.

Reo took a deep breath. First those guys muttering about Carly Day, then Leanne acting self-conscious. She couldn't wait to see how the rest of the day turned out.

Fortunately, the rest of her shift was uneventful. Before she knew it, she was sitting on the library reading rug, the billowy skirt of her dress spread around her, reading aloud.

"The end." She smiled at the young children seated around her on the bright red rug as she closed *Maybe You Should Fly a Jet! Maybe You Should be a Vet!* Dr. Seuss' book about careers always filled the children's imaginations with visions of exciting futures.

"Read again!" A tiny girl who couldn't have been more than two toddled over to Reo and pounded on the book.

"Tanika, stop." The girl's older brother trotted up and gently took her little hands in his. "I want to be a lepidopterist," he said shyly.

They were so cute! Reo nodded. "You want to study butterflies. That is so cool. What do the rest of you want to do?"

"Fireman!"

"Dancer!"

"Doctor!"

The children all yelled at once, causing the parents sitting around the circle to burst out laughing. Reo asked the children to take turns. She didn't know what was funnier, the way the children acted out what they wanted to be or the parents' expressions when their children surprised them with their choices.

"You are so good with kids," one of the women told Reo as everyone filed out.

Reo smiled, warmed by the compliment. She loved sharing her joy of reading as much as she loved working with kids. "Wednesday afternoon story time is so much fun. I'm so glad Miss Emma asked me to fill in."

The sounds of squeals and running feet echoed around them. "It takes a young person to keep up with children," Miss Emma said as they walked towards the lobby. "You'll be a great teacher one day."

"You're great with them, too," Reo exclaimed, throwing her arm around Miss Emma's shoulders. "When I was little, I loved story time with you." Her father had brought her to story time every chance he'd gotten.

Miss Emma smiled. "That may be. But my days of sitting cross-legged on the reading rug are long gone."

Reo touched Miss Emma's shoulder as the group dispersed. "I was wondering. Would you help me practice interviewing for my teaching job? Sunny said she'd help, too."

"Of course, dear. When's your interview?"

"I haven't heard yet. But I'm sure it will be soon."

Miss Emma patted her hand. "Just let me know when." She hurried off to the circulation desk where a line of patrons had formed.

Reo glanced at the clock. Almost five. She headed for the meeting room, curious to see how far the Girl Scouts had gotten on their quilting project.

The girls stood together staring at the array of patchwork squares arranged on the meeting room table. "We're working on the layout," Natalie West, the troop leader, said. She blew her auburn bangs out of her eyes. "I'm much better at hanging drywall."

"Is there a badge for that?" Reo asked her friend who worked for her father's home improvement company.

Natalie grinned. "No, but there should be."

Reo smiled as she examined the intricate designs, admiring the brightly colored fabrics and tidy stitching. Each hand-sewn square commemorated a building or an event in Lilac's history. The town hall. The library. St. Andrew's church.

"Look." One of the scouts handed her two quilt squares. "We have two for the high school."

Reo set the squares side by side as she examined the needlework. "Perfect! One for how the school looked when it was first built and one for how it looks now after all the renovations." The solar plant owner had presented a substantial gift to the town for the purpose of modernizing the high school. It now boasted a new technology building and an expanded auditorium to hold the growing student body.

Reo stepped back to study the layout of all the squares. Something wasn't quite right. While every image was a little work of art, they were too close together for the viewer to take in the detail depicted in each. "You may want to add a few more solid squares to offset the different scenes you've created," she suggested.

A big smile spread across Natalie's face. "You're right. It's too crowded the way we've done it."

Reo retrieved some sheets of blank paper from the computer printer. "Here. Pretend these are squares of white fabric. Lay them out like a checkerboard. That will set off each of your quilted squares."

Reo smiled as the girls huddled around the table, rearranging the squares until they were happy with the new design.

"That was a great idea," one of the girls said, studying the new layout.

"You're welcome. And before boxing up the quilt squares, let's take a picture so everyone can remember how you've laid them out." Reo lined up the troop along one side of the table, their quilt squares spread before them, and snapped the picture with Natalie's phone. "Here you go."

"Thanks." Natalie smiled. "I've been meaning to ask. Fred Rufalo's out of town and he usually gives the applied science badge talk. Any ideas for a replacement?"

"Not Mr. Zoeller?" The middle school science teacher was the obvious choice.

Natalie's voice dropped to just above a whisper. "The girls all have class with him already. I was hoping we could get someone different."

"Hmm. I could call—" She'd almost said Principal Owens. But she didn't want to be asking the principal for any favors until after she'd had her job interview and the Main Street decorations were decided once and for all. "You could call Principal Owens. Or call the solar plant. I bet one of the engineers would love to give the talk."

Natalie grinned. "Great suggestions. Thanks!"

After the girls packed up their supplies and left, Reo went around and closed all the windows to help Miss Emma lock up for the day. The circulation desk phone rang. Reo picked it up. "Lilac Library. May I help you?"

"Emma Farquar, please."

Harlan Howell! She'd recognize that gruff voice anywhere. She waved Miss Emma over. "It's Harlan," she whispered.

"Hello," Miss Emma said, her voice sounding guarded. After the way Harlan had avoided Miss Emma at Filmore Hardware, Reo couldn't blame her for being cautious. She watched as Miss Emma's face transformed from an expression of wariness to total shock.

"Yes, I think we can handle that." She was silent a few seconds longer. "Yes. Thank you. Goodbye." She hung up the phone, spun around, and whooped.

"What happened?" Reo asked.

Miss Emma clutched her heart. "You'll never believe it. Harlan wants to donate the newspaper archives to the library. He wants it indexed and made available for research and display. It's a miracle!"

"That's incredible!"

"He wants us all trained in how to handle the material. I can get someone from the main library in Richmond to help with that. His only other requirements are that I find someone to move it and that he gets to be named town archivist."

"I bet the high school coaches would help move it," Reo suggested. "Look how they helped with the 5K race."

"That's a great idea. Then I'll need town council permission to get Harlan named the town archivist."

"That shouldn't be a problem."

Ms. Emma wrung her hands. "I'm not so sure. Mayor Burgin and Harlan aren't exactly fast friends."

"What happened?"

"It's between the two of them." Miss Emma looked away.

Great. One more person who didn't get along with the mayor. Was this one of the reasons the mayor wanted to make an example of her and Jack? "Mayor Burgin asked me to work on the decoration proposal. Want me to ask him about making Harlan the town archivist?"

"Would you? He'd turn me down for sure."

Reo stared at the floor. So much for getting out of evaluating the decoration proposals. If she told Mayor Burgin she didn't want to work with Jack, then she wouldn't be able to help Miss Emma. "Think it's time everybody tried to get along?"

Miss Emma nodded. "I'm willing to try if Tom Burgin is."

Reo sighed. Now if she could only find a way to get along with Jack.

~

Arcade sirens and rock music pounded Jack's ears as he walked through the packed bowling alley. Video screens displayed electronic scoring for each lane. A cluster of flat screen TVs broadcast major league baseball games. The aroma of grilled hamburgers mingled with the scent of Italian pizza spices as he passed by the crowded neon-colored food court. He'd heard The Lanes had been remodeled, but it was still a shock. The bowling alley had seemed cavernous back in the day. Now there were fewer lanes, a flashy arcade, and glass-walled birthday party rooms. His memories were of crisp paper score sheets, molded yellow plastic benches, and the smell of old leather bowling shoes. Those were the days.

He scanned the crowd for Dewey's bowling team, seeing only groups of teenagers and young families. No league bowling here. When he reached the last lane, he turned and glanced around. Had he heard Vejay correctly?

"Jack." Vejay held open a door in the corner and motioned to him. "League play in here."

Jack stepped through the entrance and smiled. "Sweet."

Once the door clicked shut behind him, the only sounds he heard were the whir of balls speeding down the lanes and the crash of scattered pins. Teammates wearing matching bowling shirts clustered around old-time scoring tables. Results were projected overhead with vintage black-and-white projectors. Except for the lights directly over the lanes, the room was dimly lit, the conversation hushed. The smell of popcorn permeated the air.

This was more like it.

When Vejay went to take his turn, Dewey came over, wearing his Deutsch's Furniture Store shirt, and shook Jack's hand. "Folks call it Harlan's Compromise," he explained, his voice hushed so as not to disturb the bowlers. "When the owner decided to refurbish the place, Harlan paid him to block off these eight lanes for league play. And historic preservation."

Jack nodded. "Impressive. Harlan still bowling?"

"Remember what a mean bowler he was? Perfect form." Dewey pantomimed bowling with a swing of his arm, then planted his hands on his hips. "He had knee surgery a while back so he's settled for being league commissioner. Not sure why he hasn't shown up yet tonight."

One of the guys wearing a Casters shirt stood and shook Jack's hand. "Rasheed Jenkins. You probably don't remember me. Graduated a couple years behind you."

Jack smiled. "JV field goal kicker. Play in college?"

"One year. Tore my ACL and dropped out."

"Tough break." Jack had served with a number of soldiers who'd suffered that injury. Painful.

"No complaints. Got a good job at the solar plant."

"Rasheed's the night shift guy we sometimes need a substitute for, but he got somebody to cover his shift this evening," Dewey added. He introduced Jack to some of the other bowlers. "Co-ed league on Tuesdays if you're interested."

"Hey, Dewey, you're up, man," Vejay called.

Dewey motioned to the section of benches filled with onlookers. "Stick around and check out the competition. We're playing the Ringtones next week. We'll definitely need a sub."

As Jack approached the raised seating, the vintage stainless-steel snack bar at the back of the room caught his eye. He made his way to the counter. "I'll have some popcorn—unless you're still mad at me."

Reo spun around. She stood beside an old glass-front popcorn popper, her face flushed from the heat. She swiped the back of her hand across her forehead and pushed a stray lock out of her eyes. "No one's going to get any popcorn if I can't get this machine to work. The hopper lid jammed shut."

He walked around a group of kids wearing matching teen league shirts to join her behind the counter. He eased the long wooden spoon from her grasp. "May I?" He attempted to lift the hot metal hopper lid with the spoon. When it didn't budge, he reached behind the machine and unplugged it.

"What do you think?" She gripped his arm and peered around his shoulder.

Her hair smelled like wildflowers. Jack tried to focus on what to do next. He stepped away from the machine and set down the spoon. "You scoop the popcorn that's already popped into bags for the customers. I'll find some tools and fix this."

Relief filled her face. "Thanks, Jack."

He walked out to his truck and grabbed his tool box, protectiveness surging through him. Why wasn't anyone helping Reo? Manning that counter and taking care of all those customers required a minimum of two workers. There had to be at least ten kids waiting for Reo to serve them. Coordinating the 5K race, evaluating the decoration proposals, and now helping out with the bowling league. If he didn't know better, he'd think people were taking advantage of her.

By the time he returned to the snack bar, the old metal popper had cooled down enough to be touched. A group of teens stood around the counter chatting with Reo. From the looks on their faces, the kids were perfectly at ease with her, no small feat for an adult interacting with teenagers these days.

"Sorry for the wait," he heard Reo tell some of the kids. "We hope to have more popcorn soon."

"Assuming the repairman is up to the challenge," he tossed over his shoulder as he got out his screwdriver.

"What do you think?" Reo asked. "Is our repairman up to the challenge?"

"I don't know," one kid replied. "That's a pretty old machine."

"Well, he's a pretty old repairman," Reo quipped.

He bit back a smile as he spotted the loose screw causing the problem. "I'll get you for that one."

Reo cocked her head. "Uh-huh. I hear you."

He exhaled as he tightened the screw, relieved to hear Reo teasing him again. She'd been furious about his interfering last night. He shot her a sideways glance. Maybe he had gone a little too far, bringing her dad and Leanne out to the parking lot. But one thing he'd learned as a mediator was that the sooner these types of issues were dealt with, the better.

"Guess what? No need to talk with Harlan tonight. He called Miss Emma today." Her voice sparkled with excitement as she peered over his shoulder. "Said he'd give the newspaper archives to the library if she found a way to move it and he was—"

"—named the town archivist," Jack finished, turning so that his face was inches from hers.

Reo's eyes flew wide. "How did you know?"

Had her lips always been so full and pink? He cleared his throat and straightened. "Met with Harlan this morning and worked out the deal. Try now."

Reo stood still, giving him a look that turned his

insides to mush.

His face felt hot. "What? You've got customers." He gestured to the kids standing at the counter.

She pressed her lips together in a little smile and turned on the machine. It popped to life.

Dewey walked up to the counter. "Hey, Reo, I need four sodas, two with ice and two without."

"Sure thing." Reo pulled four cups from the dispenser. "How's your dad doing?"

"Same, pretty much. But he's starting to have trouble remembering names." Dewey's worried expression transformed into a smirk as he caught Jack's eye. "I'm all for historical preservation, man, but broke is broke. I've been telling Harlan we need to trash that popper and get a new one."

Jack closed his tool box. "A screw came lose. Nothing that couldn't be fixed."

Reo flashed Jack a smile of gratitude and handed the tray of drinks to Dewey. "Here you go. Two with ice and two without."

Jack stored his toolbox on a shelf below the counter and washed his hands. A white cook's apron hung on a peg next to the sink. He tied it around his waist and looked at the next customer in line. "What'll you have?"

Reo spun around, shocked. "What're you doing?"

"Helping." He grinned. "What else?"

Chapter Seven

An hour later, when the teams finished up their games, Reo stored away supplies while Jack shut down the popper and cleaned it. She'd been tired when she'd arrived at the bowling alley after working at the DMV and volunteering at the library. But the past hour of laughing with Jack and the customers had given her a surge of energy.

"How about a game?" Jack asked as he untied his apron and hung it on the peg.

"You're on."

After a trip to the shoe counter, Reo sat next to Jack on a yellow plastic bench and slipped on her bowling shoes. She studied his profile, the plane of his cheek, the strong curve of his chin. He didn't have to fix the popcorn machine. He didn't have to help behind the counter. He didn't have to work out the deal with Harlan. And yet he'd done all these things without being asked. Maybe she'd been wrong to assume he'd simply camouflaged his wild streak. Maybe he really had changed.

"Veterans first." She reached for a score sheet and wrote their names at the top.

Jack selected a ball. "Haven't bowled since I was in Texas."

She tapped the pencil on the page. "Don't expect mercy just because you're out of practice."

He grinned. "Guess I'll risk the humiliation."

She tilted her head. "Your work keeps you so busy there's no time for bowling?" Or dating? She watched as Jack strode to the line and threw his first ball, his tee shirt stretched tight across his muscled shoulders. Why did her mouth suddenly feel dry?

He stood silently watching until the ball smashed into the pins. He turned around, his expression smug. "Still got it."

"You rolled a split. Good luck with that." She cocked her head. "You didn't answer my question."

"What question?" He waited for the automatic ball return to send up another ball.

"About being busy."

"Sometimes the hours are long." He rolled again, wincing as the ball picked off a single pin on the far right. "Darn. Nine."

She laughed. "You might want to get some pointers from Dewey before you start subbing." She wasn't about to admit she hadn't bowled since the annual Girl Scout bowling fundraiser last fall.

Jack rubbed his shoulder. "Did he teach you?"

"No. Dad did. How about you?"

"Same. It was one of the few things my father and I did together."

She searched her memory. "I never really got to

know your dad."

"Most folks didn't. He wasn't around a lot." He sat on the bench. "When he'd get home from a trip, we'd come over here and bowl. Realize now it was his way of reconnecting with me. Doing something we both enjoyed."

Her heart tugged for the boy who had missed his father. If he'd experienced anything like the sadness that had pierced her heart when Carly Day left, it must've been awful. She swallowed the lump in her throat. "It's great you two could do that together."

"Yeah." His voice sounded faraway. "Besides bowling, all he wanted to hear about was how I was doing at football."

No wonder that football scholarship had meant so much. She escaped to the ball return, lifted each ball before choosing the one she wanted. "You need to think about the weight, you know. Use different ones depending on the situation."

"Like choosing your weapon." The corner of Jack's mouth curved up.

"Now that sounds very military. No, more like weighing your options, figuring out what works for you." She rolled the ball in her palms.

"Have you?"

"Have I what?"

"Figured out what works for you?" he asked, his tone suddenly serious.

His quizzical gaze set her stomach to fluttering. She hurried to the line, certain that Jack was not asking her about bowling. She swung her arm back and threw the ball so hard it didn't hit the lane until it was half way to the pins. Her breath hitched as the ball rolled straight and fast. "Come on. Come on. Strike!" She whirled around, arms in the air.

Jack looked at the ceiling and shook his head. "Beginner's luck."

She smoothed her skirt, ignoring his dismissive tone as adrenaline pumped through her. "Beginner? I told you. I'm a pro."

"Uh-huh."

She perched on the chair and wrote her score. "I don't remember seeing you at the Midnight Rock and Bowl. As I recall the football players were too cool for that."

Jack cleared his throat. "I managed to make it a few times." He sent two balls in quick succession, spinning straight down the lane. "Spare. How's your brother Buck doing?"

She marked the score sheet, surprised that Jack would bring up her older half-brother who'd lived with her and Donnie until he was eighteen. "Buck? Good, I guess. He owns a tour boat business in New Orleans."

Jack dropped into the seat beside her and looked around. "You know, Buck's father showed up here one night."

Buck's father Spike showed up at the bowling alley? Reo couldn't believe it. No one had told her that the biker who'd been the father of Carly Day's second child had visited him in Lilac. "First I heard of that."

"Took Buck for a ride on his motorcycle, brought him back, and drove off."

"At least he came back for a visit." She regretted the bitter words as soon as they were out of her mouth.

Jack's expression turned serious. "I take it your mom never came back."

"Oh, she came back." She tasted bitterness on her tongue. "Just not to see me."

Jack remained silent.

She stared at the floor. "When I was little, sometimes I'd come home from school and there'd be a new doll on the front porch or a game. She'd leave things for Buck, too. Baseballs. Model cars."

Jack reached for her hand, wrapping his warm fingers around hers.

Her chest tightened as images of Carly Day flashed in her mind. Setting food on the table. Folding laundry. Reading a good night story. Emotions she'd kept locked away threatened now to overwhelm her. Emotions that had nothing to do with Jack holding her hand.

Oh, God, did he feel sorry for her?

She forced a smile, tried to make her voice bright. "You know, Miss Emma always claimed she would've been a terrible mother. That's why she never married."

"No way! Miss Emma was the best. Every single teacher let me know exactly how much I'd let them down by losing my scholarship. But not Miss Emma. She was the only one who didn't make me feel like a failure."

He'd lost that scholarship because of her. Words of apology lodged in her throat. "So that's why you made that crack about teachers." She eased her hand out of Jack's and walked to the ball return. "I see what you're doing. Getting all serious to throw me off my game."

"Did it work?" Jack extended his legs and stretched his arms along the back of the bench.

"Nope." She reached for a ball and took her turn. "Come on. Come on. Strike!"

She won the first game. Jack won the second.

"You can thank me later for letting you win," she said as he walked her out to her car.

"Everything go okay at the DMV?" he asked as they crossed the empty parking lot.

"It was a little weird. Leanne was super polite. Guess I'll have to get used to it."

"Still mad at me for interfering?" He stared at her intently.

"As long as you don't say I told you so, we'll be fine." She leaned against her car door. "Guess I blew it out of proportion."

"You were shocked at seeing Donnie and Leanne together." He placed his hand against the roof, so close to her shoulder she could feel the heat coming off his skin.

She cleared her throat. "We need to get this Main Street decoration thing settled."

"I know." His gaze searched her face.

Heat spread up her back. "Since Miss Emma and the mayor don't get along, I told her I'd talked to him about making Harlan the town archivist."

"Interesting. I volunteered to talk with the mayor about Harlan's proposal to build an assisted living facility in Lilac." He tucked a lock of hair behind her ear. "Harlan claims the mayor didn't like the idea because he didn't think of it first."

His light touch sent a shiver down her neck. "That's the same thing Miss Emma said about the mayor when she suggested the 5K race."

The moon disappeared behind a cloud, casting them both into shadow. "This has suddenly turned into a lot more than just selecting a Main Street decoration proposal." His gaze settled on her lips. "Not sure it's wise to stir things up."

Her heart pounded in her throat. The intensity in his voice told her he wasn't just talking about the town. "Not wise at all." Her voice came out in a whisper.

They stood together, gazes locked, as if each were afraid to move. After a moment, he stepped back and shoved his hands in his pockets. "Guess we need to see Lavinia tomorrow."

She gave her head a shake. "Lavinia? Sure. What time?"

"Ten?"

She nodded and climbed into her car. "Good night." She could see him in her rearview mirror, watching as she drove away.

When she arrived home the house was dark, her Dad's car nowhere in sight. Another date with Leanne. She sat on the front porch, the cool breeze caressing her skin. The tree frogs croaked, punctuating the chirping crickets.

She'd wanted Jack to kiss her.

~

Jack kicked his way out of his sleeping bag and sat on the cot he'd set up in his old bedroom. Moonlight streamed through the window, checker-boarding the wood floor with squares of light. He reached for his phone and tapped open the email from the director of Peacetalkers. *The events of early May will be discussed at the hearing. We will review your responses at that time. Please submit your completed questionnaire as soon as possible.*

First, a leave of absence. Then a formal investigation. Now a hearing. And he still didn't know how to answer those questions.

He tapped the flapping wings icon on the phone screen. *Reo12.* He'd told Reo about the incident, but he hadn't told her everything. Should he tell her the whole story? Would she understand?

He walked through the streaming moonlight to the window. If he completed that questionnaire he might lose his job. Not to mention lose Reo. He closed his eyes, seeing again the look on her face when he'd almost kissed her. Somehow, since returning to Lilac he'd come to think there might be something between them. The idea scared the heck out of him. Up until now, when it came to dating, he tried to keep things light and easy while he figured out his future. But there was nothing light and easy about Reo. She seemed to see right through him and made no effort to hide her thoughts.

He suddenly knew exactly what she'd think if she found out what had really happened in D.C. She'd think he was as reckless and impulsive as ever.

He raked his hand through his hair. How had things gotten to this point? He watched a cat dart across the front lawn and back into the shadows. What would his father say if he were still alive? Not that his father had ever discussed any of the challenges he'd faced as a soldier. He'd been a master at leaving things unsaid. Unwilling to share the details of his life as a Ranger, Sean Warfield had tucked his family away in this tidy mountain home and pretended their lives were normal. How many times had his father sat with him on the front porch, sidestepping Jack's questions about the military, wanting to talk instead about Jack's latest success on the football field? Frustrated by his father's refusal to open up, Jack finally stopped asking, telling himself he didn't care. When his father suddenly died, all Jack had left were unanswered questions tangled up with grief for the man whose opinion had mattered so much.

He flipped open his laptop. Time to face the music. Question one.

He awoke with a start. The sky outside the window was just beginning to lighten. He pushed his hair out of his eyes. At some point during the night, between I-can't-believe-I-did-this and maybe-I-shouldn't-write-that, he'd closed his laptop and fallen onto his cot. Awkward didn't begin to describe how it felt, laying out his flawed decision making for the Peacetalkers to read. And he hadn't even gotten through all the questions. Getting everything off his chest was the only way to move forward, but did it have to be so painful?

After taking a quick shower, he got dressed and headed to Main Street. The shop fronts looked like a picture postcard with the sun barely visible over the distant mountain peak. The Warfield Garage interior lights flickered on as he passed. He hadn't heard from his uncle since teasing him about Kelly Prendergast. Had he struck a nerve? Another bridge he needed to mend.

Door chimes jingled as Jack entered Filmore Hardware. Not electrical chimes but old-fashioned ones hanging on the doorknob. He inhaled the familiar scents of oil soap and fresh pine, smiling at the floor-to-ceiling wooden drawers that lined the wall behind the cash register. Mr. Filmore kept every type of nail, screw, washer, and bolt imaginable in those tiny drawers. Once when he was younger he'd tried to count all the drawers and gave up when he'd reached a hundred. How many times had he stood here wishing he could climb that ladder and glide along the shelves? Mr. Filmore must've seen that look of yearning on every kid who'd ever come into the shop.

"Keep your britches on," Mr. Filmore would tell everybody who asked for a ride on the ladder. "Not until you're ten." For many of Lilacs kids it was the highlight of their tenth birthday. Coming to Filmore Hardware and riding the ladder along the shelves was more than a tradition. It was a rite of passage. Since he and Vejay had the same August birthday, they'd met at the store first thing in the morning. Jack's dad had been overseas that day but his mom had brought him. His mother had snapped pictures and had them ready to show his dad when he got back. Old Mr. Filmore had even let him get a second ride when his dad returned.

After the bowling alley, Filmore Hardware was the place his dad had brought him the most. Selecting a block of wood for his Cub Scout pinewood derby car. Picking out his first set of screwdrivers. Searching for a bolt that fit the Christmas tree stand. Years of fixing tangible things, maintaining the quality of their home, and experiencing the satisfaction of a job well done could be traced to this century-old hardware store.

The coffee maker gurgled beside the cash register. Mr. Filmore had the first pot ready at six a.m. when the store opened and kept it fresh all day, free for anyone who wandered in, whether they were looking for a two-cent wingnut or a twenty-dollar wrench.

Jack wandered down the aisle gazing into the old glass-front wooden cases. Lures, wire, feathers, hooks, fishing line in all gauges and colors filled the display. Fishing poles and creels hung from the ceiling. You could see what was important to the residents of a town by what was front and center in the hardware store.

He passed the sandpaper display, every sheet arranged in a labeled bin, and made his way through caulking and adhesives. He'd come back for paint in a few days after he finished stripping wallpaper. Right now, he needed to focus on flooring. Nothing too fancy, just some linoleum to replace the old cracked kitchen tile. He arrived at the back of the store and stopped. A table covered with a white tablecloth was arrayed with party goods: tumblers, ice buckets, plates, bowls, and platters. A rack of folding chairs was set up beside a display of various sized portable tables. A poster on the wall showed an inflatable moon bounce for kids and a water dunking tank beneath a sign that read Party Central.

Party Central? Who was having all the parties? Jack glanced around, stunned. "Where's the flooring?" he muttered.

"May I help you?" A blonde-haired man wearing dark blue khakis and a chambray work shirt with the words Filmore Hardware embroidered on the pocket stood in the entry way to the storeroom. He looked about Jack's age, maybe a few years older.

"When did you put in a rental station?" Had Mr. Filmore finally replaced that old manual cash register, too?

"About a year ago. Interested in renting something?"

Jack's gaze moved along the back wall. Tillers, aerators, lawn mowers, chainsaws—just about every piece of equipment a person could want for a project around the house was on display beneath the Equipment Rental sign. "I might need a paint sprayer next week."

"Over here."

They walked to the opposite corner where a paint sprayer sat on the shelf near ladders, tarps, and wallpaper steamers.

Jack eyed the wide-array of products. "Hard to believe there are enough rental customers in Lilac."

"You'd be surprised. Lots of do-it-yourselfers would rather rent than purchase. That way they don't have to worry about maintenance or storage."

"Good point." Jack glanced around. "Is Mr. Filmore here?"

"He moved to Arizona a couple years back. I'm Logan Reed."

"Jack Warfield." The men shook hands. "What happened? Did he get sick?" Jack asked. The old guy had been a fixture in the town.

"After his wife died, he decided to retire. None of his kids wanted to take over the business so my partner and I bought it. I used to spend summers on Lilac Mountain with my grandparents. You might know my aunt, Eva Owens, from Allen and Eva's Organic Produce."

Jack nodded. "Guess you've heard about their harvest decoration proposal for the town's anniversary. I'm one of the proposal evaluators. Should I assume Allen and Eva's is your favorite?"

Logan shrugged. "Can't say I really care that much. Whatever decorations will bring the most customers to Lilac."

As if anyone could predict that. Jack glanced around. "I really came in to get some linoleum tile. Did you move it to a different part of the store?" In the old days flooring materials had been displayed along the back wall where floor sanders and carpet cleaners now sat.

"Try Hampton's Flooring out by the mall. I can't compete with his selection, so I discontinued the tile and put in a rental station."

"Be sure to tell Tom Hampton I sent you," Logan said.

"How do you like living in Lilac?" Jack asked as the men strolled to the front of the store. Logan struck him as educated and well-mannered, refined even. Nothing like the gruff, back-hills persona Mr. Filmore had projected.

Logan's face lit up. "I love it. The people are great. Real sense of community."

"Best of luck," Jack said as he pulled open the door. "Now that you're renting moon bounces and dunking tanks, do kids still want ladder rides?"

"Are you kidding? That's a Lilac institution." He grinned. "There's a family coming in this afternoon with ten-year-old twins."

Jack stepped outside, glad to hear Lilac kids were still getting rides on the Filmore Hardware ladder. He turned towards Warfield's Garage, paused, and then headed in the opposite direction for The Shoebox. If Pete was mad at him, he'd better bring a peace offering. He needed to mend their relationship before he was called back to D.C. Popovers should do it.

While the rest of Main Street was still waking up, inside The Shoebox was hopping. Just about every seat was filled. The smell of coffee, eggs, and sausage filled the air, making Jack's mouth water.

"What can I get you?" Lulu called from behind the counter. Her face glistened from the heat.

"Two popovers to go. And two coffees, black," Jack replied, resisting the urge to order the pancake special.

He glanced around. The mayor and his wife sat at a corner booth eating breakfast. Donnie and Leanne sat in another, laughing together about something.

"Jack!" A voice called out over the din.

He looked up and saw Dewey motioning to him. He joined Dewey at the far end of the crowded stainless-steel counter.

"So, what do you think? Ready to join the bowling league?" Dewey asked. He was dressed in a light brown suit, napkin tucked into his collar to protect his dress shirt and tie.

Jack watched Lulu wrap up the popovers and fasten lids on two take-away cups of coffee. "How can I? I don't live here."

"But you'll be coming back." Dewey nudged him in the ribs. "To see Reo."

His face felt hot. Were his feelings for Reo that obvious? Was that what everyone thought?

"Saw you two at the Yacht Club Tuesday evening," Dewey said with a grin. "And bowling last night."

"You and Reo went bowling?" Lulu set the cardboard tray holding popovers and coffee in front of him.

"Yes, indeedy, they did," a white-haired man said.

"How'd they do?" asked a second white-haired man sitting next to him.

The first man shrugged. "You could've beat him."

The second man beamed.

Jack tried not to roll his eyes.

"I talked to you about playing games." Lulu put her hands on her hips. "You're not leading Reo on, are you?"

He'd been back how long? A week? And his name

was already grist in the Lilac gossip mill. Should've skipped the peace offering and gone straight to Pete's.

He fished out his wallet and put some bills on the counter. "Nobody's leading anybody on," he said as firmly as he could. "We're evaluating the decoration proposals." He picked up the tray and strode out before Lulu could ask him anymore questions he wasn't ready to answer.

~

"Now look at this." Lavinia swiped her sapphire-ringed index finger across the rhinestone-framed tablet screen, revealing another glossy red-white-and-blue photograph. "They've shaped the inflatable Mylar into colonial candlesticks and holders. These could work."

Reo resisted the urge to put on her sunglasses. Every surface inside Sparkles Galore shimmered with light. Gleaming glass counter tops revealed trays of highly polished gems and jewelry. An ornate chandelier with at least a hundred dangling crystals directed tiny rainbows of light through the air. There were so many mirrors decorating so many surfaces that no matter where she looked she saw sparkles. And Jack.

Last night she could've sworn some silent connection had passed between them, yet this morning he'd barely spoken to her. Had she imagined it? He'd been deep in conversation with Lavinia when she'd arrived at the shop, sparing her only a nod and a one-word greeting.

"I like these," Jack replied seriously, like he actually meant what he was saying. "As well as the traditional cloth bunting."

Lavinia gestured to the Main Street scene outside the window. "The town already has plenty of bunting. We need something like these Mylar colonial tapers to brighten things up. Give it a little bling."

"But not too much bling," Jack replied.

Lavinia shook her head. "Beautiful and tasteful. That's my motto."

Reo thought she might be sick. She pointed at another image on the screen. "I kind of like Lady Liberty riding the motorcycle."

Jack shot her a look before turning to Lavinia. "What are we talking about in terms of cost?"

Lavinia grinned. "A pittance. I included high and low estimates in my proposal."

Jack shook Lavinia's hand. "I believe we have all the information we need." He turned to Reo, his expression polite. "Do you have any questions?"

How about why was Jack ignoring her? Reo managed a weak smile and shook her head. "No."

"I'm having a silver sale this weekend. Stop in. I'll give you my special friend's discount," Lavinia called as they exited the shop.

Jack looked up and down Main Street. "Might as well go to the flower shop and get this last meeting over with." He sounded weary.

Reo fell into step beside him. "Gosh, I hope this isn't taking up too much of your precious time."

He slipped on his sunglasses. "I've got a lot to do today. Strip wallpaper. Order a new stove." Bells chimed as Jack pulled open the flower shop door and held it for her.

She marched past him into the store and stopped. Beautiful flowers filled the room. Cascading blossoms everywhere she looked. Every shade of pink and lavender with touches of white and blue. Magnificent scents tickled her nose. The chimes jingled again with the click of the closing door. She sensed Jack standing directly behind her, his masculine scent cutting through the floral fragrances.

"Now where did I leave that measuring tape?" A female voice drifted from the back of the shop. Mrs. Newmacher pushed her glasses up her nose as she rooted through the sheets of green tissue and cellophane littering the counter. "I thought I put it—Oh! Good morning, Reo. Jack. The mayor said you two would be stopping by."

Jack stepped forward and shook her hand. "It's been a long time. I remember my mom bringing me here when I was a kid."

Mrs. Newmacher chuckled. "Your mother loved the scent of eucalyptus. Does she still buy it by the armful?"

"Yes, ma'am. It's all through her house in Florida."

"Ah, there it is!" Mrs. Newmacher pulled the tape measure from a spot beside the register. "I suppose you have questions about my decoration proposal."

Reo nodded. "Yes, we do."

Mrs. Newmacher motioned them forward. "Come around to my workroom."

An oversized vase filled with white lilies commanded the center of Mrs. Newmacher's worktable. "These flowers will be placed in the alcove of the chapel for a wedding rehearsal tonight. The height and width must be just so."

The vase sat on a spinning platform. Mrs. Newmacher rotated it a few inches at a time, using her measuring tape to verify the correct width from each perspective. "There. I just need to snip these." She took her scissors and trimmed a few leaves.

"I can see you're a perfectionist," Jack said, his tone sincere.

Mrs. Newmacher shook her head. "The flowers are perfect. I simply arrange them." She set down the scissors. "So, what do you think of my proposal?"

Reo's gaze shot to Jack's face. Was he going to tell Mrs. Newmacher straight out that her proposal was too expensive?

"Given the name of the town, and the fact that the founder Hamish McPhee was a botanist, your proposal would seem to be the obvious choice." He rubbed the back of his neck. "Unfortunately, the anniversary is in September when lilacs are not in bloom. So, money becomes an issue."

Mrs. Newmacher exhaled a long sigh. "Lavinia suggested I use silk flowers and not hot house lilacs. But that wouldn't be true to the idea, would it?"

Reo shook her head. "No, ma'am, it wouldn't."

Mrs. Newmacher nodded, her expression resigned. "If money is the deciding factor, then go with Lavinia's or Allen's proposal. I just thought if we wanted it to be authentic we should use lilacs."

Reo felt awful. She reached for Mrs. Newmacher's withered hand and gave it a squeeze. "If it's any consolation, I like your idea the best."

The shop door bells chimed. Mrs. Newmacher covered Reo's hand and gave it a squeeze. "Thank you dear. I need to see to my customers."

Jack strode around the table. "What are you doing?"

Reo blinked back tears. "What do you mean?"

He put his hands on his hips. "You told Mrs. Newmacher her proposal was your favorite. We're supposed to be impartial."

"Impartial? Please! The way you talked with Lavinia?" She stepped closer and wagged a finger at him. "You were practically filling out the order forms."

He captured her hand in his. "We were trying to have a serious discussion. You suggested the Statue of Liberty on a motorcycle."

"Lavinia is over the top in everything she does. Mrs. Newmacher is authentic. Unlike you." She yanked her hand out of his grasp.

He straightened as if she'd slapped him. "What's that supposed to mean?"

"Oh, I don't know. Maybe it's the way you're nice to me one minute and aloof the next." She glared at him.

"Me?" His eyes flew wide. "When I first got back, you wanted nothing to do with me."

"Duh? You ran into me."

He crossed his arms. "You acted like you hated me."

"I don't hate you." She stepped backwards, her shoulders bumping into the supply shelf. Glass containers clattered behind her.

Jack's hand shot out. He steadied a shaking vase, then rested his hand on the shelf next to her head. "You don't hate me." He repeated the words, a sense of wonder in his voice. His gaze searched her face like he was looking for the answer to some secret puzzle.

Reo tilted her face up to his, the same longing she'd felt last night surging through her. Despite the circles under his eyes, raw emotion shone in his gaze. Her fingers itched to reach out and stroke his cheek. Her breath caught.

"Eh-hem," a woman's voice said behind them.

Reo peeked around Jack's shoulder. "Mrs.

Newmacher!" She ducked under Jack's arm to escape.

Mrs. Newmacher bustled to her worktable. "No worries. Flowers do that to people." She retrieved her measuring tape, giving them both a pointed look. "You would not believe what's gone down in this shop."

As soon as Mrs. Newmacher was out of the room, Jack burst out laughing. "Did she just say we wouldn't believe *what's gone down in this shop*?"

Reo bit her lip to keep from laughing.

He grinned. "Think she'd tell us *what's gone down in this shop* if we recommend her proposal?"

Her hand shot out and gripped his arm. "You wouldn't dare."

"Don't tempt me." His gaze darkened.

Her breath caught. She released his arm and hurried past him out of the work room. She prayed no one would notice how flustered she was as they made their way outside.

He reached for her hand. "Come on."

"Where?" she asked, suddenly breathless.

"You'll see," he said, his steps determined.

"There's my car," she said as they approached Sparkles Galore. She was practically running to keep up with him.

"Hey, you two," Lavinia called from her shop door. "I just found a web site that sells red, white, and blue fire hydrant covers."

"Sounds great," Jack replied without looking.

"Text me the link," Reo called over her shoulder as they hurried past. "Careful or you'll get on Lavinia's bad side," she warned him.

He shot her a serious look. "Do I look like I care if I get on Lavinia's bad side?"

He most definitely did not.

With a quick step to the right, Jack avoided colliding with Allen and Eva Owens who were setting out bushels of apples.

"Guess what? The elementary school and middle school are going to participate in the art contest, too," Allen called after them.

"That's wonderful," Reo said between heavy breaths. "Good thing I'm not applying for jobs at those schools," she muttered.

"I heard that," Jack said.

Logan Reed stood in front of Filmore Hardware, adjusting a row of shiny red wheelbarrows to make room for a green grass seed spreader. "Hey, Jack. Find what you needed at Hampton's Flooring?"

"Haven't been yet. Let you know," Jack answered, barely breaking his stride.

"Stop!" Reo dug in her heels. "I'm not taking another step until you tell me where you're going."

Jack came to an abrupt stop and regained his footing. "Back to the scene of the crime."

"Your old apartment?" She yanked her hand out of his. "No, thank you."

He raked his hand through his hair. "This thing between us, whatever it is, we can't go forward until we settle what happened before."

So, she wasn't imagining it. Something did pass between them last night at the bowling alley and just now in the flower shop. Unexpected heat sparked inside her.

He raised his hand like a Boy Scout taking an oath. "I promise not to drag you down the stairs and kiss you."

She crossed her arms and tapped her foot. "Do I have to climb the fire escape?"

The corner of his mouth twitched. "Only if you want to."

No, she would not let him smooth talk her. She needed to stop and think clearly. Did she want to relive that moment of humiliation? Part of her screamed no. Still, was he right? Was going back to the apartment the only way to put the past behind her?

She held out her hand.

He covered it with his and resumed walking. Slower this time.

As they approached the Up Do, Reo spotted Sunny sitting on the bench by the entrance.

Sunny's jaw dropped as they approached. She quickly clamped her lips into a grin. "Hey, guys, where're you going?" she asked, her tone way too innocent.

Reo tried to pull her hand free, but Jack's grip was firm. "The love shack. Call 911 if I'm not back here in twenty minutes."

Sunny nodded as if seeing Jack dragging her best friend down the street were the most natural thing in the world. She raised her phone and snapped a quick picture. "This should look great on the Lilac social media page."

"You wouldn't dare!" Reo called over her shoulder as she jogged to keep up with Jack.

Jack lowered his head and increased his pace, as if he were on a mission. They passed the library and turned into Warfield's Garage. "Pete!" Jack barked.

Pete slid out from beneath a vehicle. "Forget something? Oh, hi, Reo."

She raised her hand and wagged her fingers at him. "How're you doing?"

"I'd be a whole lot better if Jack was the one on this creeper fixing this truck." Pete winked at her.

"Where's the key to the apartment?" Jack asked, his tone impatient.

Pete pointed to the corner. "On the hook."

Jack released her hand, strode across the garage, and retrieved the key.

"Take your time." Pete chuckled to himself as he slid under the car.

Jack led her outside to the apartment's street entrance. He slid the key into the lock and opened the door. Sunlight spilled through the transom window, lighting their way up the steps to the apartment.

"Pete stopped renting the place after I moved out," Jack said over his shoulder as he unlocked the upper door and pushed it open.

She scanned the dim interior and sniffed the stale air. How many kids had passed through here? Make that passed out here. She scanned the simple furnishings. Desk, dresser, sofa, small kitchen table with four chairs. Pieces of an old brass bed frame leaned against the wall.

He pushed open the window over the sink and flicked a light switch. The ceiling light remained dark. "Guess Pete shut off the electricity." He looked around the room. "To paraphrase Mrs. Newmacher—you wouldn't believe what went down in this apartment." He shook his head. "Kids who didn't want to go home. Kids who didn't want to grow up. I understand it now, but then? Once I had that first party, I couldn't have kept them away if I'd wanted to."

She crossed her arms. "You did a pretty good job keeping me away."

He shot her a look then strode to the far side of the room. "I was standing here, arguing with Dewey about changing the music, when I looked up and saw you."

She walked to the window by the fire escape. "I climbed up with a bunch of kids and stumbled as I stepped over the window sill. Ten seconds later you were dragging me across the floor."

"You practically gave me a heart attack." A lock of dark hair fell across his forehead, giving him the same intense look he'd had that night.

She crossed her arms. "Do you know how long it took me to get up the nerve to come here?"

"You had your reputation to think about." He cocked his head.

"Guys were hooting at us."

The corner of his mouth curved. "They knew I had a crush on you."

She rolled her eyes. "You did not."

"I told you. Pete said hands off." He leaned a shoulder against the wall and stared at the floor. "I'm not proud of the fact this was party central. In retrospect, it was downright dangerous."

She tilted her head. He did not sound like the party animal she'd envisioned. She slipped her cell phone out of her pocket, tapped the screen, and gazed at the flapping wings. "You said I owed you a story."

He dropped onto the sofa, glanced at the empty seat beside him, and sent her a questioning look.

She shook her head and sat on the window sill. "As you know, I was excluded from the party scene my last year of high school."

He grimaced. "Ouch."

"You're welcome. When I arrived at Ridgeland College I was not prepared for dorm life. Kids partying in their rooms. Loud music all night. I had a roommate who—Katie was—let's just say she treated our dorm room the same way you treated this apartment."

"Party central."

"Pretty much. I finally got up the nerve to ask Katie to party somewhere else and she turned on me. The dorms were at full capacity so I couldn't move to another room. Most nights I slept on a sofa in the student lounge area."

He straightened like a dog who'd suddenly heard a whistle. "You weren't, I mean, nobody tried to—?"

"No, no. Nothing like *that* happened. Once Katie told everyone how lame I was, guys pretty much left me alone."

His gaze softened. "That must've hurt."

She nodded. She'd been devastated by the cruel lies Katie had told about her. When people suddenly stopped talking to her, she had no way to defend herself. "One night I went into the lounge and another girl was there, crying. Her name was Bianca. She'd had an argument with her roommate and didn't have anywhere else to go. We sat and talked. I told her about how I didn't get along with Katie. She told me how homesick she was for Panama. Then she gave me the app with the flapping wings. She touched her phone to mine and the app automatically appeared on my screen. It asked me to type my first name, then it assigned a number to me. Bianca told me the app would make a fluttering sound whenever I was around people who'd helped someone through difficult times." Her eyes watered at the memory of Bianca's kindness. They were total strangers and yet they had helped each other through a terrible evening with one late night conversation. "You're the first person I've met who's had the app."

He smiled. "You should come to D.C. Your app would be going off all the time."

Her jaw dropped. "You're kidding."

"Lots of flapping wings in D.C."

Amazing to think that one little app could make a difference and bring so many people together. What if she hadn't met Bianca and gotten the app? She stared out the window. "You know, if I'd gotten into the party scene in high school, Katie and I may have become best friends. Who knows what trouble I could've gotten into?"

"Are you telling me it was a good thing I threw you out of my apartment?"

She nodded.

Jack rose and walked slowly towards her. "Last night at the bowling alley it hit me. I never would've forgiven my dad if I hadn't joined the army."

She was suddenly aware of her pulse picking up. "What do you mean?"

"He was one of those soldiers who thrived in combat. He couldn't adjust to normal life. When he talked to me, all he wanted to hear about was some daredevil play I'd made on the football field." He reached for her hand. "I may never have come to terms with my dad's behavior if I hadn't met other soldiers like him in the army. If you hadn't called the cops."

Her breath caught. If he hadn't kissed her.

Jack's lips spread in a slow smile, as if he could read

her mind. "Guess I should thank Uncle Pete." He pulled her to her feet. "Dinner tonight?"

The look on his face made her heart flip flop. He wanted to take her out. Not to talk about decorations. Not to help Miss Emma. She gulped.

"What's wrong?" he asked.

"You live in D.C. and I live here." Her excuse sounded lame even to her ears.

His thumb gently brushed her knuckles. "I can drive here on weekends."

Panic suddenly gripped her. "I'm not leaving Lilac." She straightened her shoulders, her tone defensive. "I don't want to be like my mother."

She saw the puzzled look on his face and eased her hands out of his. "My mother threw aside her family five different times to chase adventure. Each time she ran off to start a new relationship."

He tilted his head, his expression perplexed. "I'm not asking you to run off. I'm asking you to dinner."

"How long would it last? Getting together on weekends, not seeing each other all week." She paced away from him, determined to speak her piece before she lost her nerve. "At some point one of us would have to give up our job and move."

He crossed the room and stood behind her. His hands warmed her shoulders as he turned her gently to face him. "Dinner. That's all I'm asking."

Her thoughts raced. "What about you? You can't do crisis mediation here. Lilac's biggest crisis is when Eva Owens' chickens get loose and stop traffic." She shook her head. "That means you'd be giving up your career for me. I don't want that."

He looked like he was about to say something then

clamped his mouth shut. Without a word, he opened the apartment door and held it for her. Her heart sank. It was for the best. He would be leaving as soon as they made their recommendation to the town council. They walked in silence downstairs to the garage.

Pete stood in front of his computer terminal, squinting at the screen.

Jack tossed the keys. "Friday. Wallpaper. Grilling."

Pete's hand shot up and caught them. He nodded.

She squinted, blinking hard as they stepped into the sunlight, her emotions in a jumble. Jack was right, they'd needed to talk about the past and clear the air. Yet her heart squeezed at the thought of what she'd given up.

Jack turned to her. "Care to join us?"

She started. "You're asking me over, after I said I didn't want to go out with you?" That didn't make sense.

He gently cupped her cheek in his hand. "Sweetheart, we have only just begun this negotiation." The corner of his mouth curled into a slow smile. "And I don't intend to skip any steps."

Warmth tingled down her spine. Whatever she'd expected him to say, it hadn't been that.

She tried to ignore the tiny thrill shooting through her. She cleared her throat and headed down the sidewalk. "Sorry, but Sunny and Miss Emma are helping me practice my interviewing skills on Friday when the library closes."

"When's the job interview?" he asked.

"I don't know. But I want to be ready when the high school calls. You don't think—" Her voice broke. She couldn't bring herself to say it.

"I don't think what?"

She stopped walking. "You don't think Principal Owens is waiting until after we make our recommendation to schedule my interview, do you?"

He shrugged. "Can't say. But if I were trying to influence the situation, it's what I'd do. One thing I've learned as a mediator. Just about everything is negotiable."

Her shoulders slumped. Would Principal Owens really make his decision about whether to hire her based on her recommendation about his nephew's decoration proposal? She hated thinking that might be true.

As they walked in silence down the sidewalk, her cell phone rang. She glanced at the screen. "That's odd. Carsondale High School."

"Maybe they want to offer you a job."

"They already did." She tapped the phone. "Hello?"

"Reo? Principal Nguyen. I'm so glad I got a hold of you."

The underlying stress she heard in her former boss's voice made her ears perk up. "What's wrong?"

"Gina was involved in a fight."

Reo gasped. "Is she alright?"

"Yes. We're trying to determine exactly what happened." Principal Nguyen's voice lowered. "I couldn't reach Gina's father. You're next on the emergency contact card. She's never gotten into trouble before. Is she having any problems at home?"

"She." The words froze in Reo's throat as her big sister instincts did battle with her professional teacher training. Best to talk with Gina before sharing her worries with Principal Nguyen. "She mentioned something about her stepmother wanting her to babysit all the time. I'm leaving now. See you soon." She looked up to see Jack watching her, his expression concerned.

"What's wrong?"

She hurried toward Sparkles Galore where her car was parked. "My little sister, Gina. She was in a fight at school. I have to go."

Jack walked to the passenger side of her car and opened the door, gesturing for her to climb in.

"What are you doing?"

"Driving. You're upset. You shouldn't be alone."

"What about stripping wallpaper and buying a new oven?"

He slipped on his sunglasses. "That can wait."

A protest died on her lips as she nodded and dropped the keys into his hand. "Thanks." She settled into the passenger seat and tried to calm her racing heart, grateful for Jack's presence as he started the engine and pulled away from the curb.

"Has this kind of thing happened before?" he asked, his tone gentle.

"Not that I know of. I never observed her having any arguments when I did my student teaching at Carsondale High."

"Not at Lilac Mountain High?"

She shook her head. "I waited until the last day to submit my application and all the student teaching slots were already filled."

Jack shot her a look. "You didn't do that for this job application, did you?"

"Oh no. I learned my lesson. This time I submitted my application the first day Lilac Mountain posted the opening on their website."

"Good."

She clutched her hands in her lap. "From what I observed, Gina had a lot of friends. She seemed happy."

"Teen dynamics is a big part of Peacetalkers training. Are there gangs at Gina's school?"

She searched her memory. "No. At least there weren't any gangs when I was teaching there last fall."

"What did you teach?"

"American lit and English comp."

Principal Nguyen had said Gina was all right. She needed to remember that. Had Gina really been fighting? Sure, Gina could be stubborn. And when she got mad she let everyone know it. But to actually get into a physical fight? No, that was not her sister.

The squat brick school building that housed Carsondale High School appeared in the distance. Faded yellow metal rimmed the windows. Splotches of orange-red paint covered brick walls to mask spray-painted graffiti. Worn dirt trails crisscrossed the dried-up lawn.

Jack pulled into the lot and parked the car. "Do you want me to come in?"

She didn't know what she was going to learn inside. She wasn't sure she wanted to face it alone. "Would you mind?"

He gave her hand a squeeze. "I've got your back."

Principal Nguyen stood talking with the receptionist outside her office. Wearing a simple navy-blue suit with her black hair pulled back into a ponytail, she exuded calm authority. She shook Reo's hand. "I'm so glad you're here."

"This is my friend Jack Warfield. He drove me."

Principal Nguyen nodded and shook Jack's hand. "Gina's waiting in my office."

Jack gave her a smile of encouragement. "I'll wait on the bench and relive my high school nightmares."

She smiled her thanks and followed Principal Nguyen into her office.

Gina sat huddled in the corner of the sofa, holding an ice pack to her cheek. "Reo!" She raced across the room, threw her arms around her sister's neck, and burst into tears.

Reo held her close and stroked her hair. "It's all right. Tell me what happened."

"I hit my cheek on the door in the girls' bathroom."

Hit her cheek? Reo stepped back and gave her head a shake. "Principal Nguyen said there was a fight."

Gina looked down, her expression sheepish. "I didn't fight with anybody."

Reo slipped her arm around Gina's shoulders and led her to the sofa. "I'm confused." She shot a questioning look at Principal Nguyen.

Principal Nguyen took the seat behind her desk. "Gina, why don't you tell us both what happened."

"I'm telling the truth," Gina pleaded. "I was alone in the bathroom, washing my hands. Three girls came in. They told me to stay away from a boy and pushed me. That's when I hit my cheek on the door."

"Who were the girls?" Reo asked.

Gina pressed the ice pack to her cheek and stared at the floor.

"Is the boy a student here?" Principal Nguyen asked.

Gina shook her head.

Reo's thoughts raced. Were the girls warning Gina to stay away from Felipe, or someone else? "We need to know who did this."

"If I tell, it will only get worse." Gina kept her gaze glued to the floor.

"Did they threaten you?" Reo asked.

Silence.

All Reo's teacher training screamed at her to get to the bottom of this. But at the sight of her sister's bruised cheek, her heart nudged her softly towards supporting Gina until she was ready to talk. She looked at Principal Nguyen and shrugged.

Principal Nguyen folded her hands on her desk. "Carsondale High School has zero tolerance for violence. Those girls were behaving like bullies."

Gina pressed her lips tight.

"You need to tell us what happened or someone else could get hurt," Principal Nguyen said, her voice firm.

Reo gripped the arm of her chair. She had a sudden memory of the time her older half-brother Buck had come home with a broken wrist. His clothes were torn and there were scrapes all over him. It had taken Donnie more than a day to get the truth from him. Against the wishes of all their parents, Buck and his twelve-year-old friends had built an eight-foot ramp in the woods for their skateboards and bicycles. Buck was the first one injured. He didn't want to get his friends in trouble for disobeying their parents.

Reo closed her eyes. Come on, Gina. Do the right thing.

When Gina didn't respond, Principal Nguyen reached for a slip of paper and pen. "You're released from school for the rest of the day to have that bruise checked out. I'm authorizing an excused absence for tomorrow if you need to recuperate. I expect to see you in my office first thing Monday morning. I hope you'll use the next few days to think about the consequences of withholding the truth." Principal Nguyen walked to her office door and motioned to the receptionist. "Please escort Gina to her locker to get her things."

Gina left the room, head hanging low.

Reo fought the urge to follow her sister and talk some sense into her. Why wouldn't she turn in those girls?

Principal Nguyen collapsed back into her chair. "Do you know how many times a week I have to deal with this kind of thing? Can you talk with Gina, help her see that covering up those girls' behavior is wrong?"

"I'll try." Sudden memories of their mother's defiance flashed in her mind. "Gina can be stubborn."

"I understand." Principal Nguyen suddenly looked weary. "This has not been an easy day. A student was in a car accident—no one was hurt, thank God. A clogged drain in the cafeteria. Plus, one of my English teachers resigned." She tapped a piece of paper lying on her desk. "Have you thought any more about my job offer? You really connected with the students when you were here last fall."

Reo stared at her hands a long moment. "I loved working here, but—"

Principal Nguyen gave her a sympathetic smile. "I know. Lilac Mountain High School is your first choice. Your town has done an awesome job renovating the school. The new technology building is fantastic. We have nothing like that here."

"It's not the new buildings," Reo protested. "Lilac is my home."

Principal Nguyen nodded. "I understand. Carsondale

is my home. But it may interest you to know two of our teachers live in Lilac."

"Really?"

"In those new townhouses near the solar plant. Many teachers prefer to live in a different town from the one where they teach. Helps keep their personal and professional lives separate." Principal Nguyen rose to her feet. "My offer stands. We'd love to have you teach here if you ever change your mind."

"Thank you."

Gina returned, backpack slung across her shoulder, an expression of shock on her face. She raised her hand and pointed into the waiting room. "Do you know who's sitting on the detention bench?"

Jack appeared behind her in the doorway. "Is that my cue?"

Chapter Eight

Jack tapped his thumb against the steering wheel, gaze fixed on the small brick rancher. The front yard was green and trim. A red tricycle sat near the front door, a baby swing hung from an oak tree.

Reo and Gina had gone inside over thirty minutes ago. No chairs had come flying through the window, so Gina's father must not have too terrible a temper. Poor kid. She'd been so worried about her father's reaction to her bruised face that she'd begged Reo to take her directly to Lilac for the weekend. But Reo had remained firm. Gina's father was required to sign the excused absence form. He needed to know what happened.

Jack certainly could sympathize with the kid. He'd cringed when Reo had brought up the importance of telling the truth. He sat back and closed his eyes, imagining the Peacetalkers' questionnaire for the hundredth time. He needed to submit his answers to Peacetalkers just like Gina needed to tell Principal

Nguyen what happened. He never should have accepted Marco's invitation to meet alone. The rule was spelled out in black and white in the Peacetalkers' policies. Why had he ignored it?

Gina was afraid of payback from the girls who'd bullied her if she told on them. He couldn't be a hypocrite and recommend she tell the truth when he hadn't yet completed the Peacetalkers' questionnaire.

What was that joke Steve always made about conscience? Can't live with it and can't live without it.

Reo hurried to the car, pulled open the passenger door, and slid into the seat. "Thanks for waiting. Gina's dad wants to speak with her alone for a few minutes."

He searched her face. "You okay?"

"Pretty awful, but thanks for asking." She gave him a weak smile. "Gina's going to stay with me for the weekend. Her dad agreed I'd have a better chance of convincing her to tell the truth to Principal Nguyen."

Jack nodded, resisting the urge to pull Reo into his arms and comfort her. If he wanted Reo to be proud of him, he had to be proud of himself. He had to come clean with the Peacetalkers. Tonight, he would answer all their questions, submit the questionnaire, and accept the consequences.

"I hadn't realized how strained things had become at Gina's house," Reo continued. "Her dad is working overtime. Her stepmother is having a rough pregnancy. Their little boy is sick with a stomach flu. I knew there was more to the story when Gina said she wanted to drop out of school."

"She told you that?"

"Last weekend at the overlook. Right before you showed up."

"Big red flag." He inclined his head towards the house. "What about her boyfriend? Felipe? Is he inside?" During the ride from the school, Gina had admitted that Felipe was the boy that the girls had warned her about. But she still wouldn't give up the names of the girls.

She shook her head. "That's another problem. Felipe works for her father's landscaping company. Just now, when Gina told her dad what happened, she left out the part about the girls telling her to stay away from Felipe."

Uh-oh. "Does her father know she's dating one of his employees?"

"I don't think so." She sighed. "I'd forgotten how controlling her dad is. He said she can stay with me, but no going out with her friends until she tells the principal the names of those girls. If he finds out she's secretly dating one of his employees, he might ground her for life."

"Or at least until she's eighteen," he replied, his tone sober.

Reo's expression fell.

He touched her arm. "What's wrong?"

"Our mother got pregnant with our oldest brother Chris when she was eighteen."

Alarm bells went off in his head. "That's the second time today you've mentioned your mom."

Her shoulders swiveled to face him. "So?"

He heard her defensive tone, saw her posture tighten as she waited for his reply. "Nothing. I was just wondering how she's doing?"

He watched Reo's shoulders rise and fall in a resigned shrug. "How would I know? She hasn't contacted me since high school."

Ouch. "Would she want to know what's going on with Gina?"

Reo shook her head. "Far as I know, Gina hasn't seen our mother in almost ten years."

Ten years? At least when his father had gone away on those long deployments Jack had known he would be coming back. And when his father had gone away for the last time, it was death that had kept him from returning, not choice.

Reo pushed a lock of hair out of her eyes as she leaned against the window. "Gina's going to get bored sitting around my house for three days."

"You can always come over and strip wallpaper." He wagged his eyebrows at her.

She gave him a withering look.

"How about *after* we strip wallpaper? I'm firing up the grill tomorrow afternoon to feed Pete and Dewey in exchange for helping. Why don't you and Gina come over?"

She looked down at her clasped hands. "I'm still meeting Sunny and Miss Emma tomorrow to practice interview questions."

"Bring Sunny and Miss Emma, too. We can get everyone's opinions of the decoration proposals. I sure as heck don't know what to tell the town council."

She pressed a hand to her forehead. "If we recommend Allen's harvest theme, people will think I did it to get hired by Allen's uncle."

"I don't want to pick Lavinia's because it means giving in to the mayor's arm twisting."

Reo gave him a surprised look. "I thought you liked Lavinia's Mylar?"

He grinned. "I just played along because I knew you hated it."

She rolled her eyes. "And poor Mrs. Newmacher. At triple the price of the other two proposals combined, nobody'll go for her hot house lilacs."

"So, you'll be there." His voice sounded huskier than he'd intended.

She looked away as the front door of the house opened. "I really need to focus on Gina."

"But you'll come."

"I'll try."

~

Reo opened her laptop in the quiet kitchen and plugged in her earbuds to watch the online lecture for her summer class. As soon as Gina had finished helping with the dinner dishes, she'd curled up on the trundle bed in Reo's bedroom and fallen asleep. The swelling on her cheek looked like it was going down and the initial bright purple color was beginning to fade, both good signs.

With a click of the video play button, Reo started the lecture and tried to focus on the lesson. After a few minutes, she stopped the video, pulled out the ear buds, and rested her head on her arm. No use. The events of the day raced through her mind, making it impossible to concentrate. Was this what it felt like to be a parent? Anxious, worried, and frustrated? If it hadn't been for Jack, she would have gone through this day alone, feeling like a failure because she couldn't convince Gina of the importance of telling the truth. He'd been supportive and non-judgmental despite the fact that she'd refused to go out with him.

She lifted her head and stared out the window at the

night sky. The idea of dating Jack both excited and scared her. She searched her memory, trying to remember any of her friends who'd made a long-distance relationship work. She came up with no one.

The screen door opened and her father entered. "Leanne has an early morning meeting tomorrow so we had a quiet dinner. How's Gina?" He sat at the table across from her.

"Sleeping." She rolled the cord of the earbuds around her fingers. "I have a question. When you told me I should be like other girls my age, were you trying to get rid of me?"

Donnie chuckled. "No. Just feeling guilty. You did everything for me after the bus accident, even skipped a semester of college. Now I'm recovered."

"And you have Leanne."

He nodded and smiled.

She grinned, tickled to see her father being coy about his new relationship. "And here I was thinking you missed Carly Day all these years."

"I did in the beginning," Donnie admitted. "Your mother may have been born on Lilac Mountain, but she was always a little bit out of place. She seemed to be searching for something that could make her happy. Guess it wasn't here."

Wow. Maybe her dad really had forgiven Carly Day for abandoning them. She told herself she no longer cared, but that wasn't the same as forgiving. What were the odds her mother would return and clear the air the way she and Jack had? For her own part, there wasn't much to say. *I was three. Why did you leave me?* And she wasn't sure she wanted to hear the answers. But sometimes she wondered what her mother had been doing. Where she'd been. Why she kept running. Was she merely impulsive or never satisfied?

She untangled the cord from around her hand and leveled a gaze at her father. "What do you think of Jack?"

Donnie seemed to wait a minute before answering. "Sounds like he's turned his life around. From what Pete was telling me, that job of his can be dangerous."

~

She recalled her father's words the next afternoon as she approached the library. She didn't like to think about the dangerous aspects of Jack's job. How had things progressed so quickly between them? Was it only last Saturday that they'd collided right here in front of the library? Her entire body warmed at the memory.

"Do I have to come?" Gina asked as she trudged up the steps beside her. She hung her head so that a curtain of dark hair covered her bruised cheek.

Reo stopped herself before she sighed for the hundredth time that day. Patience. She needed to remember what it was like to be sixteen. Gina had bristled this morning when Reo had said they would spend the day doing schoolwork. And when Gina had asked if she could get a ride to the mall to meet with her friends, Reo had refused, inviting Gina instead to watch her practice interview skills with Sunny and Miss Emma.

"This is dumb," Gina muttered as Reo opened the library door.

"You said earlier today that you wanted to get a job this summer," Reo reminded her. "You might be asked some of the same questions during your interview."

Gina stopped. "I'll be interviewed?"

Reo resisted the urge to laugh. "Yes, you'll be interviewed."

They found Sunny and Miss Emma seated together at one of the library tables. "Ready?" Reo plopped down in the chair opposite them. "Gina's going to watch."

Gina took a seat at the next table and pulled out her phone, boredom etched on her features as she scanned the screen.

Patience. "Maybe when you're done interviewing me, we can practice interviewing Gina. She wants to get a job at the mall this summer."

"Definitely." Sunny's head bobbed up and down.

"That's a great idea," Miss Emma said with a warm smile.

"Thanks," Gina muttered. She looked up from her phone. "I mean, thank you."

"I'm ready." Reo settled into her seat. "Shoot."

Miss Emma cleared her throat and read from the paper she held in her hands. "Who is your favorite author?"

"J.K. Rowling," Reo answered without hesitation.

"In what section of the library would we find books on travel?" Miss Emma asked.

"Um. Nonfiction," Reo replied.

Miss Emma smiled sympathetically. "Can you be more specific?"

Reo shot Sunny a look, but her friend was staring at her manicured nails. "The travel section."

Miss Emma shook her head. "I was looking for the Dewey Decimal number."

Reo cleared her throat. "Sunny, do you have any

questions?"

"Well, you see, the thing is." Sunny's voice trailed off. "It's not that I don't want to help."

Reo watched her friend fidget, folding and unfolding her hands. "What's wrong?"

"I've never been interviewed before," Sunny admitted.

"What?" Reo sputtered.

"I've been working around the Up Do since I was a toddler. My parents didn't interview me."

"What about the other employees?" Reo asked.

Sunny spread her hands. "Judy has been there since before I was born, and Nadine is like my third cousin. As far as I know, Mom just called them up and asked them if they wanted jobs."

Reo sat back, dumbfounded. She looked at Miss Emma. "Don't tell me. You were never interviewed for your library position."

Miss Emma nodded. "The prior librarian, Mrs. Czarnecki, hired me when I was in high school. Once I got my library science degree, I changed from part-time to full-time." She waved the piece of paper. "These are the questions I ask applicants for library jobs."

Reo closed her eyes. Great. Now what?

Gina held up her phone. "Top one hundred interview questions," she said with a grin.

Miss Emma clapped her hands. "That's a wonderful idea."

"Awesome," Sunny exclaimed. "You go first."

Gina took a seat next to Miss Emma. "Where do you see yourself in five years?" She passed the phone to Sunny.

Reo smiled. "Here in Lilac. Teaching at Lilac

Mountain High school."

"What is your biggest challenge?" Sunny asked.

Resisting Jack. The words popped into her head with such force she almost put a hand to her mouth to keep from saying them. She squirmed in her seat. "I, um, patience. Sometimes I have a hard time being patient."

Sunny passed the phone to Miss Emma.

"How do you deal with this challenge?" Miss Emma asked, her expression serious.

Reo resisted the urge to look directly at Gina. "I take a deep breath and count to ten."

Miss Emma passed the phone to Gina who flicked her finger across the screen, scrolling through the list. "Here's a good one." Gina cleared her throat and sat up straight. "There are a hundred applicants for this job. Why should we hire you?"

Reo's jaw dropped. "Do you really think Principal Owens would ask me that?"

Sunny shrugged. "He might. Do you know how many people are applying for teaching positions?"

Reo shook her head. Some of her fellow Ridgeland College students had told her they'd also be applying to teach at Lilac Mountain High. But how many? "What was the question again?"

"Why should we hire you?" Gina repeated.

How was a person supposed to answer a question like that? "I have a teaching degree. I love working with kids."

Sunny shook her head sadly. "So does everyone else who's applying for the job. I think you need to say more."

"You've already told us you don't have any patience," Gina said.

Reo shot her a look. "I remember what it's like to be in high school. I can empathize with the students, understand the kind of things they're going through."

"Did you enjoy high school?" Miss Emma asked.

"I did until senior—look, can we try another question?" Reo asked, squirming in her seat.

Gina reached for the phone. "If you could be any animal what would you be?"

"Gina!" Reo exclaimed.

"That's what it says." Gina passed the phone to Sunny.

"Tell us about an awkward situation that occurred in a prior job and explain how you handled it," Sunny read. She giggled. "I'm sure something awkward must've happened at the DMV."

Reo tilted her head. "You mean like my dad dating my boss?"

"What?" Sunny's eyebrows shot up. "You never told me that!"

"Donnie is dating your boss?" Gina asked, confused.

"I can see Leanne and your father together." Miss Emma nodded, a smile in her voice.

Reo explained how she'd seen Donnie and Leanne practicing their Texas Two-Step at the Yacht Club earlier that week. She left out the part about sneaking out the back door.

"You went to Catfish Tuesday and didn't tell me?" Sunny sat back and crossed her arms.

"Jack asked me to go. We were hoping to find Harlan there to discuss the newspaper archives." She looked at Miss Emma. "It was Jack who convinced Harlan to donate the archives to the library."

"God bless him," Miss Emma said, her voice filled

with gratitude.

"Speaking of Jack," Reo continued, "he invited us all over to his house to eat."

"When?" Sunny asked.

"Now. This evening. He's grilling burgers for everyone who's helping him strip wallpaper and paint. Gina and I are going." She ignored Gina's surprised expression. She wasn't about to give her sister a chance to make separate plans for the evening when her father said she was grounded.

"What about your interview?" Miss Emma asked, tapping her paper. "I have a lot more questions about the Dewey Decimal System."

Reo swallowed a smile. "I think I need to do some private preparation," she said, wishing she'd done a little of that before coming over. Why hadn't the high school contacted her yet to schedule an interview? Would she appear too pushy if she called and asked? "Gina and I can practice interviewing each other at home."

They helped Miss Emma lock up the library and then hurried outside to walk the few short blocks to Jack's house.

"Principal Owens' lawn is always so green," Sunny observed as they passed his house.

Reo studied the neat cream-colored Victorian with the wrap-around porch. "When I did my student teaching at Carsondale, the principal invited all the teachers to her house for dinner each semester. I wonder if Principal Owens does that."

Miss Emma shook her head. "Faculty get-togethers are held at the school since they've completed the renovations. They have a beautiful auditorium and meeting rooms now. Have you seen the new computer classrooms yet?"

Reo nodded. She'd been blown away by the bright classrooms and shiny technology. She never dreamed somebody would build a twenty-first century learning facility right here in Lilac. She shot a look at Gina. Would her sister have more interest in learning if she transferred to Lilac Mountain High? Maybe it was time for them to have a serious discussion about the future.

"They've nearly doubled the number of faculty to keep up with the growing demand," Miss Emma continued. "Since the staff has gotten so big, Principal Owens probably couldn't fit everyone in his house if he wanted to."

"What's that noise?" Gina asked.

Fluttering. Lots of fluttering. Reo glanced at her phone. The screen was covered with flapping wings. "What in the world?" She hurried around the corner to the blue and white Cape Cod with half a dozen cars parked in front.

"That's Kelly Prendergast's car," Sunny said, pointing at the black Mustang convertible.

Reo's eyes widened. "There's Leanne's hybrid."

The sound of laughter and the smell of grilling food drew them to the backyard. Pete Warfield and Kelly Prendergast sat hunched together in lawn chairs, fascinated by whatever Dewey was showing them on his phone. Harlan sat at the picnic table, talking with her dad and Leanne.

"Dad?" Reo asked, puzzled.

"Hey, girls." Donnie rose to his feet and hugged her and Gina. "Perfect timing, ladies. We're all done painting."

"I didn't know you were helping." Her gaze moved back and forth between Donnie and Leanne who wore matching paint-spattered Filmore Hardware painter's caps. She had to admit they looked cute.

"Pete called and asked if I wanted to help," Donnie explained.

"Then Donnie asked if I wanted to help." Leanne grinned.

"By the time we got here, Jack, Dewey, and Pete had already stripped the wallpaper and sanded the walls. We finished painting in record time."

"You made it," Jack said with a big smile as he came out of the house, throwing his arms wide in welcome.

Reo wondered what it would be like to walk into the circle of those arms. She held up her phone instead. "What's this?"

Jack motioned to everyone and smiled. "Everybody here came to my rescue. Finished the job in one day. So, I gave them all the app."

"But—" Reo protested.

Jack's expression softened. "It doesn't have to be a crisis. Don't you think the more people who have it, the better?"

All this time she'd associated the app with pain and loneliness instead of with people helping each other. She nodded.

Sunny whirled around. "We helped you practice interviewing. We should get the app, too."

Reo grinned and held up her phone so that Gina, Sunny, and Miss Emma could each touch their phones to hers and get the app.

"Lots to eat. Help yourselves." Jack motioned to the platters of hamburgers, hot dogs, and corn on the cob.

She could feel Jack's gaze on her as Sunny, Gina, and Miss Emma went to fill their plates. Unlike the others, he'd obviously taken a quick shower and changed into clean jeans and a polo shirt. His wet hair glistened.

"How did it go today?" he asked softly.

She shook her head, resisting the overwhelming urge to rest her head on his shoulder. "Gina still won't tell me the names of the girls who pushed her. I wish I could convince her to do the right thing."

"Maybe somebody else can." Jack's gaze moved to a point beyond her shoulder.

She turned around to see a new guest crossing the lawn.

"Felipe!" Gina set down her plate and ran across the yard. Everyone glanced up to see the handsome young man approaching the group.

"You invited him?" Reo couldn't believe her eyes.

"Called Felipe and told him what happened. Explained we needed help convincing Gina to tell her principal the truth. And her dad."

"How did you find his phone number?"

He shrugged. "Same way I found yours."

She crossed her arms. "That's not an answer."

"I know." He grinned.

Jack was resourceful, she'd give him that. "Gina's worried her dad will fire Felipe if he finds out they're dating."

"That's a risk. But maybe facing the risk head-on is better than avoiding it," he said.

She gulped. Like the risk of having a relationship with Jack? She suddenly hated the thought of him leaving Lilac.

"Welcome," Jack called out to Felipe. "Fill your plate before it's all gone."

Gina clung to Felipe's arm as they walked across the lawn, her gaze fixed adoringly on his face.

Wasn't she afraid of getting hurt? Reo glanced over at Donnie and Leanne, happily eating together in their paint-spattered clothes. Across from them Miss Emma had taken a seat next to Harlan Howell, the two of them deep in conversation. "You have a habit of doing this kind of thing, don't you?"

"What? Bringing people together? It's what I'm trained to do." He searched her face. "Although I seem to have hit a roadblock in one negotiation."

"Is that so?"

"Yep. The other party's being intransigent. Something about distance. She's having a hard time acknowledging the real obstacle." His fingers brushed hers as he handed her a plate.

A shiver ran up her arm. "Oh, really? And what is the *real* obstacle?"

He studied her. "She spends so much time helping everyone else she forgets to do things for herself."

His words struck a chord deep inside of her. "I do things for myself," she protested weakly.

"I'm not convinced." His gaze challenged her.

When she didn't reply, his expression softened into a gentle smile.

Reo turned to the food platters and busied herself filling her plate, her face suddenly hot. How was it Jack could sense things she'd never put into words? Was that a type of mediator skill? To listen for the words that aren't spoken?

He nudged her arm. "What do you think?" he

whispered, inclining his head toward the two couples at the table.

She rolled her eyes. "I told you. I'm fine with my dad dating Leanne."

"I mean Pete and Kelly."

Her jaw dropped. "You want to fix up your uncle and Kelly?"

"Why not? Pete's lonely. She's widowed. Makes sense." The fire in the charcoal grill suddenly flamed up. "Excuse me a minute." Jack hurried over to turn the hamburgers.

She carried her plate to an empty seat at the end of the picnic table. What was the matter with her? Jack was going out of his way to help everyone. The way he looked at her made her stomach do summersaults. Was he right? Did she spend so much time doing things for others that she'd lost sight of herself?

"You and Kelly ought to try it," she overheard her father saying to Pete. "Come out dancing with Leanne and me sometime."

She watched Pete's face redden as he lifted a pitcher of lemonade and refilled his glass.

"I haven't gone dancing since before my husband died. I'd love to come along," Kelly replied, enthusiastically.

Dewey was entertaining everyone with an intense analysis of his bowling form when a car pulled up. Mayor Burgin climbed out and walked across the yard. "Ready to paint," he announced, gesturing to his worn jeans and old T-shirt.

All eyes turned to Jack.

He stepped forward and shook the mayor's hand. "We just started eating, Mayor. Why don't you join us?"

"Just finished dinner with Lavinia. She sends her regrets. Painting's not her thing." The mayor scooped a brownie off a platter and took a bite.

Jack motioned to Reo. "We're really glad you came. Thought you might want to discuss the decoration proposals with our focus group."

"Focus group?" Mayor Burgin's gaze narrowed as he turned to Reo. "I thought you two were going to figure this out."

"I—we—we're still working on it." Reo stammered. She turned her head to avoid Jack's puzzled gaze.

"I don't know why we're even discussing something as useless as decorations," Harlan sputtered. "This town needs an assisted living facility. And for some reason you don't want it." He glared at the mayor.

"Assisted living facility!" Dewey exclaimed. "That would be awesome! It's getting hard for my dad to stay with me at the store. Can't leave him home alone. A facility like that would be great."

The mayor scowled at Jack. "Young man, did you bring me here under false pretenses?"

Jack shook his head. "No, sir. We got a head start stripping wallpaper. Then others arrived a little later and finished the paint job quickly."

"Humph." The mayor swallowed the last bite of his brownie. "I'm guessing you made it an invitation for painting, knowing full well that reduced the odds Lavinia would come along."

"I extended the invitation to come over and paint to you *and* Mrs. Burgin," Jack said, his tone sincere.

Miss Emma put down her glass and rose to her feet. "While you're here, Tom, I'd like to ask a question.

Why do you have such a hard time acknowledging the ideas of others? Harlan here has made a great suggestion about an assisted living facility and you're refusing to acknowledge it. Same thing happened with my suggestion for the 5K. All good ideas do not have to start with you."

"I am well aware that all good ideas do not start with me, Emma. Why do you think I asked Reo and Jack to figure out this decoration dilemma?" Mayor Burgin brushed the crumbs from his fingers. "As for an assisted living community, come to a town council meeting, Harlan, and make your pitch. As I recall, my objection was about the site your developer picked, not the facility itself. Now if you folks will excuse me, I'm going home to enjoy this beautiful evening with my wife."

"Classic Tom." Pete shook his head as the mayor walked away. "He slipped out of that mess smoother than rain drops down a windshield."

Kelly leaned across the table towards Harlan. "Exactly what site is your developer proposing for the assisted living community?" She pulled out her cell phone and tapped open a map as she and Harlan talked real estate.

The hum of conversation filled the air. Jack dropped onto the bench next to Reo. "What happened?" he asked, his voice low. "I gave you a perfect opening to tell the mayor exactly how you felt about the decoration proposals."

She clutched her hands in her lap. "You live in D.C. I have to live with the consequences."

He searched her face, his expression disappointed. "You really believe that?"

She squirmed in her seat, attraction warring with reason. Was she afraid of disappointing, the mayor? Jack? Herself?

Sunny plopped down across from them. "Okay, you two, stop whispering."

Reo straightened, grateful for the interruption.

"I just did an informal poll about the decorations," Sunny announced. "Thought you'd like to know it's a three-way tie."

Jack threw up his hands. "Maybe Harlan's right. Discussing decorations is a waste of time. Let the shop owners decorate however they please."

"No. Definitely not." Sunny shook her head vehemently. "Reo, don't you remember that hideous orange blowup tractor Mr. Filmore put on top of the hardware store a few years back? And those flags the yoga studio hung that dripped purple die on people when it rained? We definitely need a unified theme for the two-hundred-fiftieth anniversary."

The sound of angry Spanish erupted from the corner of the yard. Felipe towered over Gina, muscled arms crossed. She glared up at him, finger pointed, angry Spanish words spilling from her lips.

Everyone stopped eating.

Chapter Nine

Reo felt like her face was on fire. Her dad shot her a panicked look as Gina's voice got even louder.

She wanted to crawl under the table. Instead she took a deep breath and swung her legs around the bench in order to stand. A warm hand on her wrist stopped her.

"My house. I'll take care of it." Jack strode across the lawn. He stood between Gina and Felipe like a football referee listening to two disputing players. When he spoke, his voice was low but authoritative. Even though Reo didn't understand what he was saying, she could tell Gina and Felipe were listening.

After a moment, Gina lowered her hand and took a step backwards. Felipe uncrossed his arms and shoved his hands in his pockets.

Sunny leaned across the table. "I didn't know Jack spoke Spanish," she whispered.

"Me either." Reo watched as Gina plopped into her chair while Jack walked with Felipe over to the picnic table.

"I apologize for the outburst." Felipe spread his hands. "One of the girls who pushed Gina is the cousin of a girl I used to date. Now Gina's mad because I never told her about my former girlfriend."

"Is that how Gina got the bruise," Sunny whispered.

Reo nodded. "Can you say anything to the girls to make them stop bullying Gina?"

"I'll try." Felipe shook Jack's hand. "Thanks for inviting me." He walked to his car, head down.

Reo shot a look at her brooding sister, stung in that moment by a sudden memory of their mother, sitting by a window, with a similar dark expression.

"Should we talk with her?" Donnie asked quietly.

She nodded. As if by unspoken agreement, the other guests got to work cleaning up as she and Donnie crossed the yard to Gina. "Are you okay?" Reo asked.

Gina didn't look at them. "No."

"Want to talk?" Donnie asked.

She dug the tip of her shoe into the grass. "Not here."

"Come on." Donnie exchanged a silent look with Leanne as Gina rose to her feet. He put his arm around Gina's shoulders and kissed Reo's cheek. "Tell Jack thanks for us."

Reo watched as Leanne joined the small group gathered around Jack saying goodnight. If she was disappointed with Donnie for taking Gina home, she didn't show it.

Dewey and Pete shook hands with Jack and left. Sunny sent Reo a questioning glance, indicating with her hands that she and Miss Emma were going to get a ride home with Harlan. Reo nodded but didn't join them.

Dusk brought the softening of the sky, the gentle chirping of crickets. She stood beneath the oak tree, watching as Jack approached.

"Is Gina okay?" he asked, his tone concerned.

She shook her head. "Dad took her home to talk. He said to say goodnight."

"Glad to hear Gina can talk with Donnie." He projected a steady calm as he nodded his approval. "Too many teenagers shut out adults."

She twisted her hands together. "I'm so sorry we ruined your evening." The anguished words burst from her lips.

A startled expression appeared on his face. "You didn't ruin the evening."

"My dad and I have seen Gina's temper. But everyone else?" She lowered her head. "I felt like crawling in a hole."

He slipped his finger beneath her chin and gently lifted her face to look at him. "You have nothing to be embarrassed about. Everyone here was a teenager once."

"It's more than that. I'm worried about Gina. She's so impulsive. She feels everything so deeply."

"What about you? How do you feel?" His gaze searched her face.

She met his gaze. "Afraid to trust what I'm feeling."

"Reo Greene afraid?" He smiled. "The girl who called the cops? Who endured the wrath of the entire senior class?"

"I only called the cops because you pushed me away," she admitted, her voice just above a whisper.

All the humor disappeared from his expression. "I won't push you away a second time."

The scent of lilacs swirled around them. Surrendering to the urge she'd been fighting since his return, she lifted up onto her toes and pressed her lips to his. His hands settled around her waist. She slid her arms around his neck and stepped closer. It hadn't been her imagination. They fit together perfectly. Just like she remembered.

When she broke off the kiss, he kept his hands on her waist. "Please tell me this means we've completed our negotiation."

She arched her brow. "Didn't you say we shouldn't skip any steps?"

"I'd like to propose a compressed time schedule."

"Oh no, you don't."

He dipped his head and smiled. "Just remember, you asked for it," he whispered, capturing her lips once more.

She leaned into him, loving the feel of his strong arms holding her close, warming places inside her that had become numb from worry—about Gina, about her job, about the decoration proposals. All those cares melted at the touch of Jack's lips on hers.

A short time later, they strolled hand-in-hand past the dozing houses, the echo of their shoes the only sound on the quiet street. She glanced at his profile, her gaze lingering on the angled planes of his cheek. He stared ahead, a determined look on his face.

"Plotting the next step of our negotiation?" she asked.

He squeezed her hand as they turned on to Main Street. "I was just thinking. Some of the Peacetalkers are cleaning up a park in D.C. tomorrow. Would you and Gina like to help?"

"What about the work you have to do on your mom's house?" she asked as they passed brightly lit shop windows.

"Thought it was gonna take all weekend to strip wallpaper and paint. With everyone pitching in, we got it done in one day." He turned the corner onto her street. "Change of scenery might do Gina good. We could squeeze in some sightseeing."

"That sounds awesome." She hadn't visited the nation's capital since a sixth-grade field trip. That day, she and Sunny had sat together on the bus, gawking at the monuments and snapping pictures.

Light shone from the living room where her dad and Gina sat, their muffled voices drifting through the open window. She and Jack walked quietly up the steps and followed the wrap-around porch to the side of the house. Her pulse beat double-time as Jack drew her into his arms and kissed her.

She pulled away and pressed her cheek to his chest. "Was that the kiss-her-silly negotiation step?" she whispered, her breath coming in gasps.

"Uh-huh." He chuckled, tracing her cheek with his finger. "Tomorrow morning? Seven a.m.?" he asked.

She nodded, hoping she hadn't been too impulsive. After tonight, whatever happened, she and Jack could never go back to being just friends.

~

Jack walked in the cool evening air, Reo's incredible kiss still warm on his lips. His heart pounded. He felt like he could run a marathon. As he turned onto Main Street his phone dinged.

You coming tomorrow?

Jack dropped onto a bench beneath a street lamp to

read Steve's text. Main Street was quiet except for a few folks strolling in and out of shops. Had Steve read the completed questionnaire? Was he disappointed?

The stars twinkled in the inky sky. He'd answered the questions truthfully. *It's in your hands now, God.* If the Peacetalkers organization was going to reprimand him for ignoring the rules, then he'd deal with it.

He typed his reply.

Yep. Bringing

He stopped typing. Bringing who? A friend and her sister? Not after tonight.

Yep. Bringing two volunteers.

He hit send. There'd be time to talk over everything with Steve tomorrow. The important thing was that Reo was coming, that she'd get a chance to see a neighborhood where he worked.

He closed his eyes, savoring the memory of her kiss. At the first touch of her lips, his pulse had kicked into overdrive. He'd forced himself to keep his hands on her waist, to take things slow despite his racing heart. She was beautiful. Smart. Her hesitation about going to dinner had startled him, but now he understood. She loved this town. He had to make it clear he would never force her to choose between Lilac and him. How the heck could he do that?

Well, Lord, since You're helping me with everything else, could you help me with Reo, too?

Sometimes he wondered if his prayers were trivial, if the things he wanted were inconsequential compared to the needs of others. An Army chaplain had told him once that God's love wasn't a zero-sum game; there were no winners and losers. Only infinite love for all.

A shop door jingled. His eyes popped open.

"I don't care," Mrs. DeStefano said, her voice sharp. "I'm not putting pumpkins and squash in a beauty salon." She pulled her pink blazer tight and buttoned it.

"There are other vegetables. And don't forget about fruit. Well, hey there, Jack!" Mr. DeStefano said.

Jack rose to his feet. "Evening, Mrs. DeStefano. Mr. DeStefano."

Sunny's parents looked like they'd gotten dressed up for a Friday night on the town. They did their best to smile, but it was clear they'd been arguing.

Mr. DeStefano shook Jack's hand. "How's it going? Glad to be back in Lilac?"

"Yes, sir."

"Have you and Reo selected a decoration proposal?" Mrs. DeStefano asked.

Jack gripped the back of his neck. "Not exactly."

Mrs. DeStefano put her hands on her hips. "Well, whatever you do, please don't pick that harvest proposal."

"Now, Betty Sue." Mr. DeStefano slipped his arm around his wife's shoulders and gave Jack an apologetic look.

"Do you have any idea how long it's taken some of us to bring a little bit of style to this town?" Her eyes flashed. "The thought of using cucumbers and radishes to decorate for our two-hundred-fiftieth anniversary just boggles the mind."

"I'm sure Jack and Reo will evaluate the proposals fairly and come up with a good recommendation. See you at the town council meeting." As Mr. DeStefano turned to go, he looked back over his shoulder and winked. "Harvest proposal."

"Vince!" Mrs. DeStefano swatted his arm.

"What? It's a free country!" Mr. DeStefano grinned. "See you, Jack."

~

Could the sun be any brighter? Reo flipped down the passenger seat visor as Jack turned eastward. Maybe now they'd get out of this awful traffic jam. Cars everywhere. People everywhere. The overwhelming smell of exhaust fumes and stale garbage made her queasy. Now she remembered why she hadn't come back to the city since sixth grade. She hated crowds. They made her feel closed in. Claustrophobic.

"I don't see any monuments," Gina grumbled from the back seat.

Since Jack's truck didn't have room for three people, they'd decided to take Reo's car. He drove slowly through a dilapidated neighborhood with crumbling sidewalks and boarded up buildings. The pot-holed pavement was lined with old row houses and metal-grated storefronts. Many buildings had broken windows and walls covered with graffiti.

"We're helping the Peacetalkers clean a park first." Reo looked out the window at the cramped buildings that seem to be piled on top of each other. She bit her lip to keep from asking if the area was safe. Just because a neighborhood was poor didn't mean it was crime-ridden. She'd learned that in her teacher training. Plus, Jack wouldn't take them to a dangerous neighborhood. Would he?

Jack reached over and squeezed her hand. "What do you think?"

There was nothing like this in Lilac. Reo gulped. "Is this the neighborhood where you work?" she asked.

"One of them," he said, his voice proud.

The car was suddenly filled with fluttering noises. "My phone screen's covered with flapping wings," Gina exclaimed.

Jack grinned. "You might want to mute that. Lots of people in the city with that app."

"Is it a church thing?" Gina asked.

"More like a good Samaritan thing," Jack said as he parked. "I've never been able to find out where it started."

"The girl who gave it to me was from Panama," Reo said. She stared at her phone, trying to read all the names. There were at least fifty, maybe closer to a hundred, flapping wings crowded into the little screen. Reo suddenly felt ashamed for feeling afraid. There were kind people here who helped others. She had no right to judge anyone's circumstances. Just as she loved Lilac and couldn't imagine living anywhere else, she was suddenly certain others felt the same way about city life.

A small group of people waited on the curb beside an open lot. Jack cut the engine and they climbed out. He shook hands with the African-American woman who stood at the head of the group. "Mrs. Kirui, this is my friend Rhiannon Greene and her sister Gina. Mrs. Kirui is the community projects organizer for this neighborhood."

Reo started at the sound of Jack's voice saying her formal name. She couldn't remember the last time anyone had called her Rhiannon. "Call me Reo."

"It's a pleasure." Mrs. Kirui shook her hand and smiled.

"About time, dude." A man dressed in torn jeans and a gray tee shirt, as tall as Jack but with hair buzzed short, pulled Jack into a hug.

Jack looked around. "Where's Patti?"

"Home with her feet up. Doctor told her no bending or lifting until after she delivers." He turned to Reo. "I'm Steve, Jack's boss."

"I'm Reo. This is my sister, Gina."

Steve smiled. "Thanks for helping today. A few more folks should be here any minute with supplies."

Reo took in the worn park benches and patchy grass covering the narrow stretch of ground. Hard to believe this was where the neighborhood children played, a tiny lot squeezed between crumbling row houses.

"What do you think?" Jack whispered.

That she used to foolishly complain about living in the smallest house in Lilac. "I've never visited a city neighborhood before," she answered truthfully.

A pickup arrived, its truck bed filled with rakes and shovels, garden gloves and trash bags. Reo spotted packages of grass seed and trays of colorful flowers, ready to plant.

"Okay, Mrs. Kirui, we're all here. What would you like us to do?" Steve asked.

"Start with picking up the trash. And watch out for broken glass," she warned. "We no sooner got that streetlight repaired when somebody shot it out again."

Gina's eyes widened. "Shot it out!"

Jack nodded as he handed out thick gardening gloves. "What some people do for kicks."

Mrs. Kirui took Gina under her wing, pointing to the spot where she wanted the bright red geraniums planted.

Jack touched Reo's arm. "You okay with raking up debris? Steve and I usually take care of the playground equipment."

She nodded and picked up a rake as Jack carried a toolbox to the swing set. She watched as he inspected all the bolts, tightening whatever was loose. Images of Lilac's municipal park with its brightly-painted merry-go-round and green athletic fields filled her mind. Children ran freely there, climbing on the jungle gyms, swinging on the swings. She'd played there as a child with no thoughts of stepping on broken glass.

When she finished raking a corner of the park, she glanced around. Jack and Steve stood at the opposite corner, talking. Jack shoved his hands into the pockets of his jeans and stared at the ground. Steve faced him with his arms crossed, shaking his head.

Embarrassed for intruding on what looked like a personal conversation, she looked away. Whatever they were talking about, it was clear both men were upset. She could only imagine the types of negotiations the Peacetalkers became involved in. Did someone else get hurt?

She separated the debris into litter and yard waste, then walked to the pickup truck to retrieve a trash bag and a compost bag.

Mrs. Kirui stood next to the truck speaking with a teenager dressed in jeans and tee shirt. Mrs. Kirui motioned for Reo to join her.

"I think she wants to help us," Mrs. Kirui said, smiling at the young woman standing with her. "I don't speak Spanish. Do you?"

Reo smiled. "I don't, but my sister does. Gina!" She motioned for Gina to join them.

Gina got up off her knees, pushing a lock of hair out of her face as she walked over. As soon as Mrs. Kirui explained, Gina and the teenager were speaking rapid Spanish.

"She's from Mexico, not far from where my grandmother lives," Gina said brightly. "Her name is Alejandrina. Her family just moved here."

"Tell Alejandrina welcome from all of us," Mrs. Kirui said with a big smile. "Tell her I'm from Kenya and that I understand what it's like to be far from home."

Reo tried to imagine leaving Lilac and going to a completely different country where she didn't speak the language. Could she do it? Could she give up all the things that were so familiar to her and be brave like this young girl and Mrs. Kirui?

Alejandrina's face filled with excitement as she and Gina continued talking. "She's going to help me plant flowers," Gina announced as the two girls headed for the flower bed.

"I'm so glad Gina was here to translate," Mrs. Kirui said as Reo pulled the bags she needed from the truck bed.

"Me, too," Reo said. "Although Jack could have helped. He speaks Spanish."

"But Jack's not a teenager." Mrs. Kirui looked to where the two girls worked, chatting and giggling as they planted flowers. "They speak their own language. Jack tells me you want to be a high school teacher."

Reo nodded, surprised Mrs. Kirui knew. "I'll be starting in the fall."

Mrs. Kirui nodded her approval. "Children need good role models. Oh, look," Mrs. Kirui lowered her voice. "Gina is giving Alejandrina the angel app."

Reo turned just in time to see the girls touching their

phones. A lump formed in her throat as she watched them smile and hug.

Thank you, God.

Reo cleared her throat. "Is that what you call it? The angel app?"

Mrs. Kirui smiled. "It's a good name, don't you think?"

Reo thought about that as she returned to work, raking up the debris. She knew what angels were. They weren't man-made and they certainly didn't live inside cell phones. But if someone could create an app like this, that reminded people how to help each other, she knew that was a good thing. And like Jack had told her last night, the more people who had it, the better.

She glanced over to where Jack and Steve were working. They'd moved on to the sliding boards, tightening bolts and wiping off the metal. They worked together easily, like they'd done it a thousand times before. They'd served in the army together. Her face suddenly felt warm. Had Jack told Steve that Reo was the one who'd called the cops on him? That she was the one who'd ruined his chances of attending college?

"Want a drink?" Gina appeared beside her holding two bottles of water.

Reo accepted the bottle and drank deeply. "The flowers you two planted look nice."

"Thanks. Alejandrina had to leave, but we're going to talk later." Gina pressed the cold bottle to her cheek. "Can you see the bruise?"

"It's fading," Reo said.

"Alejandrina asked me if my boyfriend hit me."

"What did you say?" Reo asked.

"I told her, no, my boyfriend's ex-girlfriend's

cousin." She grinned. "We laughed at how stupid that sounds."

Reo touched Gina's arm. "Still mad at me for making you come?"

Gina shook her head.

By noon they'd finished planting flowers, spreading mulch, and repairing the equipment.

"Thanks for your help," Mrs. Kirui said as the volunteers loaded up the rakes and tools.

"See you next month. Thanks for coming, everybody." Steve shook Mrs. Kirui's hand, then Reo's and Gina's. He turned to Jack. "See you Monday," he said with a somber look.

Jack nodded, his expression serious, and shook his hand.

"What's on Monday?" Reo asked as they walked to the car. Gina walked ahead of them, checking her phone.

"The Peacetalkers' board wants to discuss that incident I mentioned," he replied, his voice low.

Was that what Jack and Steve had been talking about while they'd been working on the equipment? From the expressions on their faces when they'd been speaking, it hadn't looked like good news. "Is everything okay?" she asked.

"Just thinking about how good I'll feel once Tuesday gets here. Don't forget," he added, "we've got the town council meeting Monday night."

"You'll be back from D.C. in time?" she asked.

"Oh yeah. The town council meeting isn't until seven. Hey, I promised you both some sightseeing," he announced as they reached the car.

Gina looked down at her dirt-smudged knees and

stained shirt. "I feel gross. I don't want to walk around like this."

"I have an idea," Jack said as he climbed in and started the engine. "Let's get takeout food for lunch and tour the main monuments by car."

Reo nodded. She didn't feel much like walking around either after all that work. She turned to her sister. "What do you think?"

"As long as we get something to eat," Gina replied. "I'm starving."

Jack seemed to know where all the best food trucks were and the quickest ways to get to them. Reo couldn't believe how well he knew the city. He drove around the block multiple times while Reo and Gina stood in line to get fish tacos and waited patiently whenever they got out in front of a monument to snap selfies. The Washington Monument. The Jefferson Memorial. The Lincoln Memorial. Reo had forgotten how magnificent they looked in person.

By early evening they were cruising down the interstate, not too far from Lilac. Soft music played on the radio as Gina dozed in the back seat. Reo glanced at Jack's profile. What a perfect day they'd had.

He looked at her and smiled.

She gulped, suddenly realizing that she wanted to see Jack's smile every day. What was going to happen when he went back to work?

The sun painted the sky shades of pink and gold as they turned off the highway onto the road that led into town. Pink, white, and purple lilacs lined both sides of the winding country lane. Reo checked her phone. "Still no email from the high school."

"Have any of your friends from college gotten calls

from Lilac Mountain High?" he asked.

"If they have, they haven't told me." She turned and stared out the window, trying to remember how many of her classmates had talked about applying. Maybe one or two, but she hadn't talked to all the education majors.

Jack parked the car in front of Reo's house. "Maybe the principal wants to wait until June to start calling applicants."

"I hope so." Reo reached into the back seat and touched Gina's arm. "We're home."

"Oh." Gina awoke with a start. "Good. I need a shower. Thanks, Jack." She climbed out of the car and headed into the house.

"Think she had a good time?" Jack asked.

Reo hesitated. "I think so," she said finally.

His brow furrowed. "Did you?"

She stared straight ahead. "It's so crowded in the city," she said, searching for the right words.

"And?" he asked.

"I really liked helping and cleaning the park," she said.

"But?"

"It felt like everything was crowding in on me. Maybe I'm claustrophobic. I could never live there," she said, her voice sad. "I can tell you love the city, though." And probably don't want to ever leave it.

Jack blew out a breath, a hint of frustration in his gaze. "We're taking things slow, remember? I invited you and Gina along to help. I wasn't trying to convince you to leave Lilac."

"I know, it's just—"

He gripped her hands. "We haven't even reached the

I-like-video-games-and-you-don't stage. Can't we just take it a day at a time?" He ran his thumb across the back of her hand. "How about we practice you kissing me and me not pushing you away again?"

She laughed, shocked she could find humor in a situation that suddenly seemed so hopeless. One day at a time. Could she do it?

"Sure, I can't interest you in installing kitchen tile tomorrow?" The corner of his mouth tugged upward.

"I have to take Gina home. Her dad invited me to stay for lunch." Helping Jack with his kitchen floor suddenly sounded much more appealing than spending the afternoon at Gina's house. Her father would be expecting Gina to go to school on Monday and tell the truth to the principal. She pushed away the thought. "You and I have to figure out what we're going to tell the town council Monday night."

He rested his forehead against hers. "Think anybody would notice if we skipped it?"

She started, shocked he'd even suggest that. "You wouldn't dare."

"Why not? Neither of us has an answer." He raised her hand to his lips and planted a kiss on her knuckle. "Guess we'll have to go through the getting-embarrassed-in-public-together step."

The touch of his lips against her skin sent goosebumps down her arm. "Not one of my favorite negotiation steps," she said.

"Mine either. But, seriously, maybe somebody else at the meeting will have a suggestion."

Just give up? She didn't like the sound of that. The mayor had asked them to come up with a solution. "We still have two more days," she said, her voice determined. "We'll think of something."

He folded his arms around her. "If you say so."

Reo pulled away. "You don't sound convinced."

He raked his hand through his hair. "We've had a week. Neither of us has an answer. At this point we just might need a miracle."

Reo thought about Jack's words the next morning as she sat between her father and Gina in church. *I know it's not a big problem, Lord, but please help us come up with a solution for the town council,* she prayed silently. Ever since she'd been a child, she'd never doubted that the Lord heard her. She knew He always answered prayers, maybe not exactly the way she wanted, but always for the best. *And please watch over the neighborhood we visited yesterday,* she added, feeling guilty for telling Jack she didn't like the city. Had she been wrong to say she could never live there? Did that make her a selfish person?

After church, she drove Gina back to Carsondale.

"I've decided to tell Papa and Principal Nguyen the truth," Gina announced as they passed Carsondale High School.

Reo gave her sister a grateful smile. Another prayer answered. The Lord certainly did work in mysterious ways. "That's great. What made you change your mind?"

"I thought about what Principal Nguyen said. Those girls were acting like bullies. If I don't say something, they might try to bully someone else."

Reo's heart burst with joy as she parked in front of Gina's house. "I'm so proud of you."

Gina shrugged. "Besides, I broke up with Felipe. It doesn't matter to me if my father fires him."

A chill ran down Reo's back. "You *want* Felipe to get in trouble?" Her sister couldn't be that cold hearted.

"Why should I care?" Gina tossed her head. "He didn't tell me about his old girlfriend. That means I can't trust him."

"But you're telling the truth to hurt Felipe," Reo sputtered.

"So?"

"That means you're doing the right thing for the wrong reason." Couldn't Gina see that was wrong?

"You called the police on Jack because he threw you out of his party. Isn't that the same thing?" She crossed her arms.

Reo opened her mouth to deny it, then clamped her lips shut.

Gina fluffed her hair. "Besides, I'm not like you. I don't care what people think."

"What's that supposed to mean?" Reo asked, her throat tight.

Gina counted on her fingers. "Everyone likes you. You're always nice. You never argue with anyone."

"That's not true! I'm arguing with you right now," Reo exclaimed, while a small voice inside her prodded, *Isn't it?*

"I can't believe this!" Gina threw open the car door. "I'm telling the truth. Why aren't you happy?" She slammed the door and headed into the house.

Oh, Lord, Reo prayed. *What do I do now?*

Reo closed her eyes, imagining again the rush of fury she'd felt all those years ago when Jack had kissed her and then thrown her out. She'd called the police and felt so proud of doing the right thing. She'd shown him. He deserved to get in trouble for rejecting her. And for a few days she'd actually believed it.

Until all the consequences of her one vengeful act came crashing down on her and everyone else. After that, she would have done anything to take back that phone call.

She'd spent her childhood trying to be good, to always do the right thing to make up for her mother's selfish behavior. After seeing the consequences of her phone call to the police, she became even more resolved to avoid conflict, to put the needs of others before her own. Yet even in that behavior she'd gone to extremes, just as Jack had pointed out.

Help me understand. I thought we were supposed to put others first.

Chapter Ten

Jack tugged at his collar, wishing he hadn't knotted his tie so tightly, wishing he was anywhere but here. The commute from Lilac through rainy, Monday morning rush hour traffic had only served to darken his mood. Instead of a two-and-a-half-hour drive into D.C., it had taken him over three hours, making him ten minutes late for the meeting.

Tardiness was not going to help his case.

Of course, lying awake half the night hadn't helped. Something nagged at his conscience. It wasn't until well after midnight that he realized he should've told Reo the whole truth. After they'd finished cleaning the park, he'd had the perfect opportunity to tell her how he'd ignored the rules and gotten injured, but he'd chickened out. He may have answered every question on the Peacetalkers' questionnaire honestly and submitted it, but he'd been ashamed to tell Reo the truth. Would she go back to hating him when he did?

The three-person Peacetalkers review panel sat

before him. Steve had sat, silent, against the wall the entire time the board had discussed his answers, displeasure written all over his face.

Did Steve regret recommending him for the job?

The woman sitting in the center of the table put on her glasses and shuffled some papers. "So, you accepted Marco's invitation even though it was against Peacetalkers' policy to attend a negotiation alone."

"Yes, ma'am," Jack answered.

"You knew you were breaking Peacetalkers' policy?"

Jack stared straight ahead so he wouldn't have to see the disappointment on Steve's face. "Yes, ma'am."

Right. Wrong. Consequences. He could hear Reo's voice saying that to him. "I knew the Peacetalkers' policy. I knew I wasn't supposed to meet with Marco alone."

"I see. Could you tell us why you went?" she asked.

Jack sighed. Moment of truth. "I guess I wanted to prove myself."

She removed her glasses, her glance filled with sympathy. "New employees often want to show they're up for any challenge. The only problem is Marco knows our policies. He knew you weren't allowed to meet with him alone."

His breath sledgehammered out of his lungs. "It was a test."

She nodded sadly.

How could he have missed that? He should have known! Why hadn't Steve warned him? Cold certainty shot through him. Because Peacetalkers needed to know if Jack could pass the test.

Obviously, he couldn't.

This wasn't about proving himself on the football field. Real lives were at stake. He was too impulsive, too eager to get the kind of attention he used to get from his father.

"It's unfortunate you didn't tell Steve what you were thinking. If you had, you would have learned there was already an ongoing investigation into the soup kitchen activity and that by meeting Marco alone you might endanger people." She tapped her pen on the tabletop. "You realize the young man who attacked you has now disappeared."

"No, ma'am, I didn't know." The cold feeling spread in his stomach. "I did offer to go to the police with him."

"Which would have been another violation of our policy," the man sitting beside her said, frustration in his voice. "No one communicates with the police alone. We must preserve Peacetalker neutrality at all times if we are to be trusted by all negotiating parties. There are reasons we have the policies we do."

"To prevent idiots like me from getting stabbed," Jack said, a bitter taste in his mouth.

"Not only that," the woman answered. "To protect the integrity of our organization."

The man sitting on the other end of the table who hadn't said a word scribbled on a piece of paper and slid it in front of the woman. She looked at the note, her expression quizzical. After a moment, she lifted her shoulders in a slow shrug. "Negotiation requires training combined with a certain temperament. It took a lot of courage to come here and tell us the truth. Not many people can admit when they're wrong and accept the consequences."

Her acknowledgment of his frankness did nothing to assuage his disappointment in himself. *Please give me another chance.*

The woman stood. "Now if you'll excuse us, the board has a decision to make."

~

Reo strode into the town hall Monday evening. She'd been thinking all day about it. She'd made up her mind about the proposal. She needed to tell Jack, convince him it was the right thing to do.

The air vibrated with the thrum of voices. Over a hundred people filled the hall. She scanned the crowd for Jack as she headed for the front row. Oh my. The DeStefano family was taking this seriously. Sunny, dressed in lilac chiffon, sat between her mother who wore a stars-and-stripes jacket and her father who sported a John Deere tractor cap. Other town residents were similarly decked out in farming overalls, patriotic gear, or shades of purple.

"I haven't seen this much rivalry since the wood-versus-metal playground equipment debate," Mrs. Newmacher said as Reo took a front row seat beside her.

"Wood won," Allen Owens said with a self-satisfied tone, his wife Eva nodding beside him.

"This is so exciting," Lavinia gushed, diamond rings sparkling as she waved two miniature American flags. She took the empty seat next to Eva.

Reo's stomach suddenly felt hollow. Where was Jack? Why hadn't he answered her text? Had his meeting run over? She needed to tell him what she'd decided and find out if he agreed.

Mayor Burgin took his seat at the center of the long

table facing the crowd. The other members of the town council sat to his left and his right. He tapped the microphone. "Thank you all for coming to the town council meeting. First item on the agenda is a discussion regarding preparations for the town's two-hundred-and-fiftieth anniversary. Reo, are you ready to make your recommendation?"

She stood and glanced around. "I was hoping Jack would be here." A feeling of dread settled on her as she remembered their last conversation. Was he upset because she'd told him she didn't like the city? He wouldn't intentionally skip the meeting because she'd disappointed him, would he? He said he'd be back.

Mayor Burgin waved his hand. "Jack called to say he might be late. He told me his recommendation. I'd like to hear yours first."

What? Jack made a choice and didn't tell her? How could he do that? She stiffened. "I thought you wanted us to come up with a single recommendation?"

"Yes, that was my original request. But given these unforeseen circumstances, we can discuss both suggestions separately."

Great. She looked down the row of expectant faces. Mrs. Newmacher. Allen Owens. Lavinia Burgin. She stiffened her spine, preparing to disappoint two of the proposal submitters. Both Gina and Jack were right. She was a people pleaser. She'd sat up half the night reading about people who got into the habit of putting others first and losing sight of their own needs.

The other half of the night she'd prayed for strength. While she'd been trying all these years to love your neighbor as yourself, she'd left out the loving yourself part.

Her determination wavered as the impact of what she was about to do hit her. If she disappointed people she cared about, they wouldn't turn against her, would they?

She took a deep breath. She had to say what she believed, even if people didn't like it, even if it contradicted what Jack picked. "I recommend Mrs. Newmacher's lilacs proposal."

The room erupted with cheers and shouts. Mrs. Newmacher reached over and squeezed Reo's hand. Mayor Burgin looked away.

"I can't believe you didn't pick my proposal." Lavinia pointed her flag at Reo, her bright red lips in a pout. "Aren't you patriotic?"

Reo cringed. "Of course, I'm patriotic. But we have patriotic displays for Memorial Day, the Fourth of July, and Labor Day already."

Lavinia tossed her head, her sparkly dangle earrings swinging back and forth. "You can never have too much red, white, and blue."

"Lavinia's proposal was the cheapest," a town council member called out, his tone displeased.

"No one said money was the deciding factor," Reo replied, her heart pounding in her throat.

"Money is always a factor," Allen Owens spoke up. "Which is why my proposal makes the most sense. Produce is abundant in September."

Reo forced herself to face him. "I admit it's the right time of year. But the town is called Lilac, not Harvest."

Allen crossed his arms and scowled. "Knew you wouldn't pick mine. Admit it. You were afraid folks would accuse you of playing favorites to get on my uncle's good side."

Silence fell over the room. She glanced over her shoulder. Sunny, sitting between her two stern-faced parents, gave her a thumbs up. Reo took deep breath. "I did apply to teach at Lilac Mountain High School where your uncle is principal. But I still like Mrs. Newmacher's proposal better."

"May I say something?" Principal Owens rose to his feet and cleared his throat. "Favoritism is not an issue. Reo isn't eligible to teach at Lilac Mountain High for another year."

"Not eligible?" Reo's knees almost gave out. "But I submitted my job application before the deadline."

Principal Owens spread his hands. "Yes, but you haven't graduated. All applicants must have completed their college degrees by June."

"Oh." Reo's face burned. She whirled around. Her father stared at her with a look of dismay. He already felt guilty because she'd delayed her degree by dropping out to take care of him. She clenched her hands. She'd been so focused on the application submission deadline that she completely missed the college degree requirement.

Mayor Burgin gave her a curt nod. "Thank you, Reo."

She dropped into her seat. She wouldn't be teaching at Lilac Mountain High. One little class had prevented her from graduating and getting the job of her dreams. One little class she wouldn't have overlooked if she hadn't been volunteering so much. If she hadn't been organizing the 5K race. If she hadn't been so focused on pleasing everyone. She squeezed her eyes shut.

The mayor banged his gavel. "Now I'd like everyone to hear Jack's recommendation."

Reo's breath hitched in her throat. Which proposal did Jack pick?

"I have been accused lately of taking credit for other people's ideas." Mayor Burgin gave Miss Emma a pointed look. "I want to make it perfectly clear that this idea is Jack's. As soon as I heard it, I knew it was a winner. Are you ready? Jack said we should use all three."

Reo's jaw dropped. "All three?"

The room exploded with cheers.

~

Jack yanked the town hall side door open to the sound of hoots and hollers. At least somebody was happy.

"Think about it," Mayor Burgin's voice boomed over the crowd. "Why limit the town to one day of celebrating? We can start in May with the lilacs. Natural lilacs grown right here that'll hardly cost a cent. Move on to red, white, and blue decorations for the summer patriotic holidays. End with the harvest theme on the actual anniversary date."

"Perfect!" Allen Owens called out, jumping to his feet. "The town can celebrate from May to September. Think of all the foot traffic on Main Street. Guess it took somebody like Jack to find the best solution."

What? Jack's feet were frozen in place as his gaze searched the crowd. Uncle Pete stood with Dewey, laughing. Miss Emma sat next to Harlan who clutched a large cardboard tube to his chest, scowling. Donnie and Leanne talked quietly, heads close together, their expressions solemn.

Where was Reo?

Sunny's parents rushed to his side. Vince DeStefano

grabbed Jack's hand and gave it a shake. "Finally. Peaceful meals again." He threw his arm around Jack's shoulders and led him to the front of the room.

Lavinia squealed as she threw her arms around Jack and kissed his cheek. "I just knew you'd come up with a great idea." She gave him an extra tight squeeze and then trotted off.

People crowded around him, pounding his back and congratulating him. He spotted Reo off to the side, arms crossed, legs crossed. Sunny sat with her, speaking softly. Mrs. Newmacher stood over them, a worried expression on her face.

"Excuse me." He broke away from the crowd and slipped into an empty folding chair next to Reo. "What's wrong?"

"Nothing." She stared at the floor as if she were waiting for it to open up and swallow her.

He pointed. "Your foot's jiggling."

She scowled at him.

"She's mad the mayor liked your idea better than hers." Dewey dropped into a nearby seat and punched him in the arm. "Way to go, bro. You nailed it."

"Shut up, Dewey." Sunny grabbed Dewey's sleeve and tugged him away. Mrs. Newmacher followed.

Jack waited until he and Reo were alone. "What was your idea?" he asked politely.

"Mrs. Newmacher's lilacs." Reo stressed every syllable, her voice stiffer than a rusted pump handle.

Jack nodded. "Principled."

Her foot bobbed up and down even faster. "Just not as good as yours."

"Which, by the way, was an angry retort to the tune of, 'I don't care if you use all three!'"

Her foot stilled.

The breath eased from his lungs. "When it looked like the Peacetalkers' hearing was going to run long, they let me make one quick phone call. I called the mayor. I should've called you."

"Would've been nice." She resumed staring at the floor.

He hated that he'd let her down, that he hadn't been here for her. He glanced around. Sunny stood to the side with her parents, watching them, her expression concerned. Donnie sent him a questioning glance: *Can I trust you to take it from here?*

He straightened. For today? Tomorrow? Forever? That would be up to Reo. She may not want him after she learned what happened.

He held Donnie's gaze and nodded.

"How did the hearing go?" she asked finally as the crowd thinned around them.

Moment of truth. "I got fired."

Now she was looking at him. He hated seeing the shock on her face, hated worse that he'd put it there. He leaned forward, elbows on his knees. "What you said before, about me being impulsive and stirring up trouble, was true. It cost me my job."

"Join the club."

He straightened. "What did you say?"

"I said, 'Join the club.'" Her blue eyes flashed. "Don't sit there all pouty-faced expecting me to pity you. I'm sick and tired of putting everybody's feelings before mine. It cost me my job." Her foot started jiggling again.

Pouty-faced? He cleared his throat. "Care to elaborate on that?"

Lavinia scurried over. "I didn't mean it when I questioned your patriotism, Reo honey. I was hurt you didn't pick my proposal. You understand, don't you?"

Reo gave her a stony look.

Lavinia wrung her hands. "I know." Her face lit up. "Come by the shop tomorrow. I'll give you the earrings that match that pretty silver necklace you were wearing the other day."

"Give them to Sunny. It's her necklace," Reo replied.

Jack fought to keep a straight face as Lavinia scuttled off.

Allen Owens approached, John Deere hat clutched in his hand. "I never should've said what I did about favoritism. You picked the lilac proposal because you liked it." When Reo didn't reply, he turned around and gave his hand a frantic wave.

Principal Owens hurried over. "Put my foot in my mouth, saying you weren't eligible to teach because you hadn't graduated." He leaned close. "You're not going to file some kind of personnel grievance against me, are you?"

Reo studied her fingernails. "It would have been nice to learn I wasn't eligible to teach earlier." She looked up. "In private."

Jack gave a low whistle as the Owens men trotted away. "I missed all that?"

Reo blew a lock of hair out of her eyes. "Those were the high points."

Mayor Burgin rapped his gavel. "This meeting is adjourned."

"What about the assisted living facility?" Miss Emma called out. Harlan stood grim-faced beside her.

"Next time," Mayor Burgin called over his shoulder as he filed out with the members of the town council.

Jack caught Harlan's eye as he walked past. He stood and held out his hand. "Next time?"

Harlan nodded, his expression determined, and gave Jack's hand a shake. "You betcha."

Jack dropped back into his seat and tried his best not to look pouty-faced as he waited for Reo to make the next move. He'd let her down. She had every reason to be mad.

She turned, finally, and really looked at him.

He saw the sadness beneath the bravado and shook his head. "I abandoned you. I'm sorry."

She bent forward and buried her face in her hands. "I hate that word."

"What? Sorry?"

"No. Abandoned." She lifted her distressed gaze to his. "You were right about me putting everyone else's needs before my own. Guess you know people-pleasing behavior goes hand-in-hand with childhood abandonment."

"Yeah, they kinda go over that in Peacetalkers' training." He hated seeing the raw sadness in her eyes. He wanted nothing more than to pull her into his arms and comfort her. Instead, he held up his phone so she could see the screen filled with silver wings. "Can't say you're abandoned now. Donnie, Leanne, Sunny, Miss Emma. Even Dewey. Everyone we gave the app to is waiting outside to make sure you're all right."

They stared at the tiny screen, a microcosm of what Reo loved most about Lilac. The people who'd supported her when her mother left. The people who'd encouraged her to get involved and stay in school. He made a silent vow to himself that he would never, ever, ask her to choose between him and the people who meant so much to her.

"We're supposed to love our neighbors as ourselves. I truly believe that," she said quietly. "Somehow I forgot about the love yourself part." She leaned her head against his shoulder as they watched the tiny silver wings. "I'm sorry about your job."

He exhaled the breath he'd been holding and covered her hand with his. "I deserved to get fired. I intentionally broke the rules trying to prove myself. I was afraid if I told you, you'd think I was still impulsive."

She shifted, angling her face up to him. "Are you?"

He could get lost forever in those blue eyes. "Yep."

Her lips quivered. "I'll always be a people pleaser."

"Good." He slid his arm around her shoulders and drew her close. "Maybe we can swap faults sometime."

She chuckled. "Now *that* would be interesting."

Jack closed his eyes. *Thank you, God.* "Pete will be happy I'm back in Lilac. Will you?"

She snuggled closer. "Guess that depends on how our negotiation goes."

Epilogue

"We haven't had snow on Thanksgiving in twenty years," Pete said as he took his winter coat off the peg and opened the front door. "You coming with me to pick up Kelly?"

Jack sat on his uncle's sofa, reading the news on his laptop. He shook his head. "Think I'll walk, thanks. See you at Donnie's house." He'd been staying with Pete the past week while the wood floors in his house were being refinished. A messy job he'd been happy to contract out to Hampton's Flooring.

His house. He smiled. His mom had been overjoyed when he said he wanted to buy her rental house and move in. Both she and Pete had done a decent job of pretending not to be too happy when he'd told them he was no longer a Peacetalkers mediator. He'd moved back to Lilac and been working at Warfield's Garage for a few weeks when Peacetalkers called and offered him a job as a motivational speaker. He'd been stunned. They wanted him to travel to schools and tell his story with the hope he'd inspire young people to overcome adversity and avoid some of the mistakes he'd made.

And maybe one day, the Peacetalkers told him, he could resume his mediator training.

He'd jumped at their offer, grateful to them for giving him a second chance. Since he was traveling to schools all over Virginia, it was just as easy to live in Lilac as it was to live in D.C. On days when he wasn't visiting schools, he worked with Pete at the garage. He'd never be the top-notch mechanic that Pete was, but working with his uncle again helped him realize that keeping the Warfield's Garage in the family was important. He liked to think his father would have wanted that, too.

Slipping on his coat, he patted the pocket. The tiny velvet box was still there. He'd sworn Lavinia to secrecy two weeks before when he'd gone to her shop to look at rings. After Lavinia invited Sunny, Mrs. DeStefano, Miss Emma, Mrs. Newmacher, and Leanne to consult on ring styles, he'd feared keeping it a surprise would be darn near impossible. But somehow, they'd managed it. The women assured him Reo had no idea.

And that she'd love it.

Tiny snowflakes swirled around him as he headed towards Main Street. Just like the unexpected Thanksgiving snow, a lot of things had happened that he never could have predicted. The desperate gang member who'd attacked him emerged from hiding and turned himself in to the police. Pete, a confirmed bachelor, was dating Kelly Prendergast. And his friends Steve and Patti had still wanted him to be Steve Junior's godfather.

Even Reo, who'd had her heart set on teaching in Lilac, loved teaching at Carsondale High School where Gina was a senior. And who could've predicted that he and Reo would now have weekly fault swapping days, where she got to be impulsive and he got to please others? So far, he'd used his people pleasing time organizing volunteers to help move the newspaper archives from Harlan's house to the library. It had taken Reo a while to get the hang of being impulsive, but it wasn't too long before she was kidnapping him from the garage and taking him on surprise picnics and mystery hikes.

He smiled. *Well, God, since You're so good at making things work out, could You give Reo and me some time alone today?*

That might just be asking for a miracle. At least twenty people were coming to Donnie's house for Thanksgiving. Reo was probably going crazy getting things ready, fussing about every detail and loving every minute. He'd never met anyone who could do so many things at once. It wasn't just her energy that was amazing. It was the love she brought to everything she did.

The love she'd brought into his life.

As he reached the house, the front door flew open. Reo hurried down the front steps, red dress swirling above the tops of her black boots as she slipped on her coat. She grabbed his hand. "Come on. We have to go get cream."

"What?"

"For the mashed potatoes. I could've sworn I bought some last week, but I can't find it." Snowflakes glistened on her streaming blond hair as she pulled him towards the sidewalk.

Jack shot a glance over his shoulder. Leanne, Sunny, and Mrs. DeStefano stood inside the open front door, grinning. Sunny pulled the container of cream from behind her back and waved it at him.

"Reo." He came to a dead stop, the importance of what he was about to do deepening his voice to a solemn tone.

She whirled around. "Should we walk or drive?"

"Neither." He took a step towards her.

"But we need—"

He slipped the ring box from his pocket and opened it. "Will you marry me?" He held his breath.

Her jaw dropped.

Clearly the women had kept his secret.

Her eyes sparkled as the snow swirled around them. "Score one for impulsive."

He grinned. "Think I'll have another chance today?"

She shook her head. "It's beautiful." She reached up and touched his cheek. "Are you sure you're happy in Lilac?"

"Yep."

"And you don't mind all my volunteering?"

He turned his face and kissed her palm. "As long as the kids and I can come along."

"Will—Oh!" she said in the breathless voice he loved. Her cheeks turned an adorable shade of pink. "How many?"

"Four. You know, for a bowling team."

Her beautiful lips curved into a smile. "Yes, I'll marry you." She held out her hand.

He slipped the ring onto her finger, smiling at the explosion of hoots and cheers as the woman he loved with all his heart wrapped her arms around his neck and kissed him.

THE END

This is Pamela Ferguson's debut novel

Visit pamelaferguson.com to sign up for my **newsletter** to read about my upcoming books.

Also by Pamela Ferguson:

One Lilac Christmas (A Lilac Historical Romance)

December 1943. When Zachary Flynn suggested that he and Amity Belmont enlist together, he never dreamed the recruiters would reject him because of his flat feet. Now, Amity's off fighting the war, and he could kick himself for letting his bruised ego get in the way of telling her his true feelings. If he had, maybe Lilac's well-meaning matchmakers wouldn't be trying to hustle him under the mistletoe with someone other than Amity.

Sergeant Amity Belmont never should have confided her fears to anyone in her Women's Army Corps unit. When her commanding officer gets wind of Amity's concerns, she recommends Amity set things right at home before taking on her new assignment. Of all the people she's disappointed, Amity is worried most about Zach. She cannot ask him to forgive something she doesn't regret. Will her surprise visit to Lilac bring the Christmas miracle they both need? Find out what happens in *One Lilac Christmas*.

Award-winning author PAMELA FERGUSON writes romantic suspense and contemporary and historical romance fiction. *Wings of Love*, her first novel set in the fictional town of Lilac, won a 2017 Romance Writers of America Golden Heart® Award. Readers can meet relatives of her contemporary Lilac characters in her World War II-era historical romances. She collaborates with professional voice artists to create audiobooks for all her books. In 2021 she began the HACKLE COUNTY romantic suspense series.

If you enjoyed this book, please consider posting reviews on Amazon or Goodreads. Thank you!

Enjoy other books by Pamela Ferguson

ROMANTIC SUSPENSE

Hackle County
Time Will Tell, Book I

SWEET ROMANCE

Lilac Contemporary Romances
Wings of Love, Book 1
True Hearts, Book 2
Mercy Me, Book 3
Red Bows and Mistletoe, Book 4
Christmas at Mountain Mist, Book 5
Love Accepted, Book 6
A Little Christmas Spirit, Book 7

Lilac Historical Romances

His Scottish War Bride, Book 1
His French War Bride: Normandy, Book 2
One Lilac Christmas, Book 3

You'll love reading Sunny and Buck's love story in Book 2, *True Hearts*. Here's the first chapter. Enjoy!

Chapter One

Sunny DeStefano popped open a can of Hard to Hold and doused Lavinia Burgin's bright red locks with enough hair spray to freeze a basket of slithering copperheads. She gave the styling chair a spin and smiled at Lavinia's reflection. "Sleep with a satin pillow case. Your hair will be perfect tomorrow."

Lavinia fanned the aerosol fumes with crimson-tipped fingers, diamonds flashing on her hands and wrists. "What we endure for beauty," she pronounced with a dramatic sigh, rising from the chair and glancing around the salon like a queen surveying her kingdom.

Sunny brushed off her hands and headed for the cash register before Lavinia could see her lips pull into a grin. Too bad it was only country music playing in the background and not *Pomp and Circumstance*. As the mayor's wife and owner of Lilac's only jewelry store, Lavinia had a fondness for dramatic gestures and all things sparkly.

"I see you've made some changes," Lavinia gestured to the reception area's new curtains and brightly-colored lilac cushions. "Did your mother approve?"

Sunny bit her tongue and counted to ten. "I'm going to surprise her."

"She'll be surprised all right. These colors are definitely

not Betty Sue's style." Lavinia pulled out her wallet. "You know, your parents were just a teensy bit worried about retiring and leaving you in charge. Not that you're not capable," she added hastily. "It's just that you're so young. I was thirty and married before I opened Sparkles Galore."

"Really?" Sunny's lips pulled into her polite-hair-dresser smile. Her father had been more than ready to retire to Florida after his sudden heart attack. Unfortunately, from the number of calls Sunny received from her Mom each day, it was clear somebody was having trouble adjusting to the move.

"I promised your parents I'd keep an eye on you." Lavinia wagged her finger playfully.

"I'm sure my mom and dad appreciate everything you and the mayor do for Lilac." Sunny swiped the credit card. She was getting way too much practice talking with a clenched jaw. "Are you going to Donnie and Leanne's wedding rehearsal party?"

"Of course. We try to accept every invitation. It's our duty to the residents who so kindly elected Tom into office." Lavinia lifted her chin as she surveyed her profile in the mirror. "Although, I'd be just as happy to skip this particular event."

"How come?" Sunny's brow furrowed. Donnie Greene and his bride-to-be Leanne Killian had invited the entire town to a cook-out this evening, the kick-off event for a weekend full of celebrating.

Lavinia patted her hair into place. "Don't get me wrong. I know you and Donnie's daughter Reo have been best friends since kindergarten. But just between you and me, those siblings of hers leave something to be desired."

Sunny stiffened. "What do you mean?"

"Don't pretend you don't know." Lavinia took a compact from her purse and applied some pressed powder to her shiny nose. "From what I hear, Gina's constantly moving in with different family members. Buck works in the swamps. Chris defends the worst kind of criminals. Nobody even knows where Devlin is. Carly Day's children are all as impulsive as she is."

Sunny gripped the edge of the counter, the tension from remaining silent coiling in her stomach. People were going to gossip about a woman who had five children by five different men. She knew that. But it wasn't fair that Reo and her half-siblings had to endure the consequences of their mother's choices their entire lives. How many times had Sunny been required to follow her mom's edict and stand by silently while customers traded stories about her friends?

Well, her mom wasn't running things anymore. Sunny lifted her chin. "I love Reo and her family."

"Those brothers are certainly handsome, there's no denying that. But dependable? Not in a million years." Lavinia snapped her compact shut. "Your mother used to worry you'd get involved with one of them. Don't give me that look. She almost had a cow when Buck Day invited you to prom."

"Reo's siblings are my friends," Sunny replied, her jaw tense. "As for getting involved, Reo's brothers live elsewhere. My business is here in Lilac."

"Right you are. We business owners need to stick together for the good of the town." Lavinia patted Sunny's hand. "Speaking of which, have you decided what specials the Up Do is going to offer for the two-hundred-fiftieth anniversary celebration?"

Rats! How could she have forgotten again? Her mother

had called just yesterday to remind her. "I'm still finalizing my list. When do you need it?"

"By the first of July." Lavinia sighed. "You don't know how much I miss having you on the beautification committee. You were such a big help. I wish you hadn't dropped out."

Sunny missed helping the town council, too. But with Mom caring for Dad around the clock and Sunny managing the shop single-handedly, there'd been no time for volunteer work. "Maybe another time."

"I certainly hope so. We need dedicated young people like you to serve." The entrance chimes jingled as Lavinia opened the door. "Oh my, I wonder who that is." She nodded towards the shiny black sports car idling at the curb.

Sunny's jaw dropped. She'd never seen such a beautiful car. Long and low to the ground, it dominated Main Street, purring like a sleek black cat. "Wedding guest?"

Lavinia's eyes widened. "Maybe they'll be shopping for jewelry." She scurried outside.

Sunny watched as the sports car's passenger door swung open. An unexpected clash of angry shouts pierced the quiet street. Gina and Buck! She'd know those voices anywhere.

Gina, dressed in a short denim skirt and tie-dyed tank top, sprung from the car onto the sidewalk. Her brother Buck, his blue eyes blazing, leaned across the passenger seat and glared at his sister. "They're expecting us."

Gina crossed her arms. "I told you. No."

Lavinia turned around to watch the scene, eyes rounded with interest.

Uh-oh. Sunny had never seen Buck so angry. Not even the time she and Reo had filled his hiking boots with styling mousse.

Sunny ran forward and pulled Gina into her arms before either sibling could say another angry word. "Gina! How are you?"

"Sunny!" Gina sounded relieved, her slender arms squeezing Sunny tight.

Sunny motioned towards the shop. "Come on in. I'm just locking up." She waited until Gina disappeared inside the salon before leaning down to the open car door.

"What do you think you're doing?" Buck demanded.

Impatience only intensified his masculine features, making the angles of his cheekbones sharper, the set of his jaw more determined. With his long dark hair and electric blue eyes, he looked like one of those medieval warriors in the action movies her dad liked to watch.

Sunny pasted a sweet smile on her face. "You can thank me later." She waved to Lavinia.

Lavinia waved back then continued into her shop.

Buck scowled. "For what? Keeping up appearances with someone I don't give a—"

"See you at the cook out." Sunny jumped back and slammed the passenger door. The sports car revved to life and roared away from the curb. What was Buck thinking, getting into an argument with Gina right on Main Street? Didn't he know people like Lavinia craved episodes like that to gossip about?

Sunny brushed her hair out of her eyes as she entered the shop, trying to calm her pounding heart. "Hope you don't mind, but Buck just left."

Gina sat in a black leather styling chair, primping in the mirror. She waved her hand dismissively. "He does that kind of thing all the time."

Buck abandoned his sister on the sidewalk all the time?

That didn't sound right. True, Buck could be ornery, and he used to disappear for days at a time when he was a teenager. When it came to his other sister, Reo, he'd always been there for her. Didn't he treat Gina the same way?

Gina spun her chair around and laughed. "I just wanted to get out of the car. We've been driving all day." With her black hair pulled back in a ponytail, Gina looked like all the other high school girls who walked past the shop window each day—bright-eyed and full of life.

"Where from?" Sunny hurried around the shop, turning off equipment.

"New Orleans. I'm living at Buck's place."

"How's that working out?" Buck had always been the silent type—except when he disagreed with someone. And he and Sunny had disagreed a lot.

Gina shrugged. "I work at the tour boat refreshment stand."

In the middle of the swamp? "You'll have to tell me about New Orleans. I've never been." Sunny threw open the door to the small rear office and scanned the desk to make sure nothing needed to be put away. She printed the register totals and counted the money while Gina took down her ponytail and combed her hair. Most of the day's customers had paid with credit cards so there was little cash to slip into the bank deposit envelope. "How about we walk to the party together? I just have to make a quick stop at the ATM."

Sunny inhaled the cool mountain air as she locked up the shop. She loved this time of the day. The sun hung low in the sky, just atop the Blue Ridge Mountains, casting Main Street in a golden glow. In a little while, when dusk fell, the Victorian-style street lamps would automatically light up, making each shopfront glisten. She scurried to the ATM next door and deposited the money.

Gina leaned against the brick wall, studying her cell phone screen while she waited.

Sunny's phone chirped. Mom's third call of the day. "Hi, Mom."

"Who's at the party?" Her mother whispered into the phone.

"Why are you whispering?" Sunny asked.

"Did Leanne's sister from Memphis show up, the one with the five-caret diamond ring?" her mother asked. "Are she and Leanne still fighting?"

Sunny blew out a breath. Mom and gossip, match made in heaven. Not. "We're just now leaving for the party."

"You and Nadine? I thought she was off today."

"Nadine was off today. I'm going with Gina." Sunny glanced at Gina and smiled.

"Gina who?" Her mother gasped. "Not Carly Day's daughter!"

"Gotta go." Sunny tapped the hang up icon. The phone slipped from her hands and clattered onto the sidewalk. She snatched up her phone, scraping her hand on the concrete. She winced.

"Is it broken?" Gina asked.

"The case is chipped." Sunny sucked on her bleeding knuckle as she examined the damaged case. If her mother hadn't called her, this wouldn't have happened. "My mother needs to get a life!"

"What?" Gina's eyes flew wide.

Sunny blew out a breath, immediately regretting her outburst. "My parents moved to Florida three months ago. My mom still calls every day to check up on me. She keeps forgetting I'm twenty-five."

Gina stared at her open-mouthed, the click of their heels on the sidewalk filling the awkward silence.

Sunny took a deep breath as they turned the corner onto Donnie's street. Guilt coursed through her. Why was getting along with her mother still so hard? They didn't even live together anymore. "I'm sorry. I shouldn't have vented like that. My mom's okay. She just misses me, I guess." Sunny forced a smile. "Are you looking forward to the party?"

Gina wrapped her arms across her stomach. "Not really. Everyone's older than me."

"There'll be some people your age," Sunny reassured her. "I bet Donnie and Reo can't wait to see you."

Gina didn't look convinced. "Reo's married to Jack now. Donnie's getting married tomorrow."

And Gina was alone. Sunny's heart squeezed. Gina didn't have to say it. Underneath the youthful exuberance, she was like so many of the teenagers who came into the Up Do. Uncertain about what they wanted or where they fit in. Not sure how to act. Sunny laid her hand on Gina's arm. "I'll stay with you at the party. Besides, we both have to eat."

The smell of grilling barbeque tickled Sunny's nose as they approached the neat blue and white Cape Cod. Guests of the bride and groom stood in groups on the lawn, their plates heaped with food. Her stomach rumbled as she called out to friends.

"See? You know everybody," Gina muttered, her voice sullen.

"I cut their hair," Sunny whispered as she waved. "If I'm not nice, they'll tell my mom."

Gina giggled.

"Gina!" Reo Warfield hurried across the lawn and pulled her sister into a hug.

Sunny smiled with relief as Gina relaxed into her sister's embrace. Reo was the kindest, most giving person Sunny knew. She couldn't believe almost a year had passed since Reo had gotten married. With Reo driving to Carsondale every day to teach and Sunny managing the Up Do here in Lilac, it had gotten hard to find time to spend together.

Reo extended her arms to Sunny. "Hey, Cinderella."

Sunny's lips pulled into a grin at the sound of her elementary school nickname. "Hey, Snow White," she replied automatically, as if they were both ten again.

Face lit with joy, Reo pulled her into a hug. Sunny blinked back the sudden moisture in her eyes. They lived in the same town, yet they hadn't seen each other in how many weeks?

"You two still call each other those nicknames?" Gina asked.

Reo winked at Sunny. "Once a princess, always a princess, right?"

"You said it, girlfriend." Sunny grinned as they bumped fists.

Gina screwed up her face. "That's weird."

Sunny put her hands on her hips. "Rhiannon Greene Warfield, didn't you tell your sister how we came up with those names."

Reo glanced around and lowered her voice. "I'm Snow White because I spent all my time taking care of everybody else's needs when I was a kid. Sunny is Cinderella because her parents had her working at the hair salon as soon as she could walk."

Sunny held up her hands. "Not that I minded."

"Maybe you didn't," Reo said with a huff. "You couldn't play with me because you had to sweep up hair. My stuffed animals and I were not amused."

Gina laughed. "Which princess would I be?"

Reo grasped her sister's shoulders and eyed her up and down. "Sleeping Beauty, because you don't see how beautiful you are inside and out."

"I'm not beautiful," Gina protested, dipping her chin.

Reo spread her hands. "See what I mean? What do you think, Cin?"

"Definitely. Sleeping Beauty." Sunny pulled out her phone and aimed it at the three of them, amazed by Reo's knack for always knowing the right thing to say to cheer someone up. "To commemorate our royal reunion." She snapped a selfie of their three smiling faces.

Reo's husband, Jack, suddenly appeared behind his wife on the tiny screen. "Me, too." He planted a kiss on the top of Reo's head as he slipped an arm around her waist. Sunny felt that sudden tug of yearning that hit whenever she was around couples who were so obviously in love. Reo and Jack were head-over-heels crazy about each other.

Sunny tried to focus on taking the picture. In the background of the selfie, she watched Reo's oldest brother, Chris, sprint across the lawn towards them.

"Don't forget me." Chris slid his lanky frame in between his sisters, bumping them each playfully on the hip. "How's it going, Sunny? Last time I saw you, you had purple hair."

Sunny laughed, relaxing into the warm feelings that Reo's family always stirred in her. "Thought I'd better tone it down for the wedding."

"That's code for better not tick off the bride, right?" Chris stretched his neck and turned his head as if he were looking to see if Leanne was in earshot.

Reo poked Chris in the side. "Sh."

"I'm the oldest. I can get away with it." Chris turned around. "Hey, Buck, get over here."

Sunny glanced over her shoulder. Buck stood talking with Donnie, his expression serious. He made a final comment to his stepfather and sauntered across the lawn.

Gina's smile faded as Buck approached. Sunny tightened her arm around Gina's shoulders, protectiveness surging through her. What was going on between Gina and Buck?

"Where do you want me?" Buck drawled.

"Stand next to Sunny," Chris commanded.

"Do I have to?" Buck asked.

Sunny pressed her lips together. She could take a hint. "I'll step out and take the picture. You guys are all family."

Buck's hand on her arm stilled her. "I was teasing." His lips eased into a smile. "Go ahead and take the picture."

A tingle shot across her skin where he touched her. Sunny glanced to her left. If she stepped away, Gina would be standing next to Buck, something Gina obviously didn't want to do. Sunny pasted a smile on her face. "Okay, on three." As everyone huddled closer, Sunny suddenly felt Buck's muscled arm around her shoulders. Her heartbeat skipped as she leaned against him, her cheek bumping his chest as his spicy scent washed over her.

"One, two, three," Sunny said, steadying her shaking hand. She snapped the picture.

Everyone gathered around to see the photo. Everyone except Buck. Without a word, he released Sunny and disappeared into the crowd.

So, he was still mad at her for interfering earlier.

"Hey, Gina, stop talking so much." Chris laughed as he lifted Gina into his arms and spun her around, making her squeal in surprise. "Race you to the food."

Sunny laughed as the two took off across the lawn. Thank goodness, Gina got along with her other brother Chris.

Reo gave Sunny's arm a playful poke. "Did you see my text? I don't have shoes to match the bridesmaid dress."

Jack slipped his arm around Reo and grinned. "You mean the pink cloud?"

"That's the polite name for it." Reo scrunched up her face, and Jack pulled her close, laughing. "Layers and layers of pink all puffed out to here." Reo spread her arms wide. "Anyway, can I borrow a pair of black patent sandals?"

Sunny crossed her arms and tapped her foot. "Sure, if you explain why you didn't tell me you're pregnant."

Reo pressed her hand to Sunny's mouth. She shot a worried glance at Jack. "I *told* you she'd know." She lowered her hand. "Promise you won't tell anyone. I don't want to upstage Dad's wedding."

"Congratulations!" Sunny whisper-squealed, pulling them both into a hug. "You mean upstage your future stepmother. Good choice. Here she comes."

"We're hungry." Reo tugged Jack's hand, pulling him away.

"Cowards," Sunny mouthed as they disappeared into the crowd.

The hem of Leanne's long floral skirt brushed the grass as she glided among the guests, making it look like she was floating across the lawn. Sunny held her breath as she studied the elaborate honey-gold up do she'd created for Leanne that morning. Still intact. Thank goodness she'd used both gel and hair spray to keep Leanne's hair under control.

Leanne squeezed Sunny's hands, her green eyes bright with purpose. "Thank you so much for agreeing to style my attendants' hair tomorrow. I don't know what I'd do without friends like you."

"I'm looking forward to it." Flowers. Dresses. Food. Photos. For almost a year, Leanne had agonized over every detail, determined her wedding would be stunning. It may have been Donnie's second wedding, but it was Leanne's first, and she wanted everything to be perfect. She'd wanted to hire wedding service providers from Charlottesville, but Donnie had put his foot down. Lilac businesses only. Sunny would never hear the end of it if she spoiled even one tiny aspect of the celebration. Not to mention what her own mother would say.

Leanne's pink lips stretched into a smile, her expression sugar-sweet. "Would you be able to do me one more favor?"

Why was Leanne holding her hands so tight? Sunny resisted the urge to step backwards. "Sure. What?"

"Give Donnie and Buck haircuts tomorrow morning."

Sunny's jaw dropped. "I thought Donnie was going to the barber shop."

"That was the original plan. Now that Buck is staying with Donnie, I thought you could drop by the house and kill two birds with one stone."

Sunny shot a glance across the lawn to where Buck stood talking with Tom and Lavinia Burgin. Her gaze narrowed. She couldn't believe Lavinia, smiling pleasantly at Buck as if she'd never said those mean things about him at the salon. Buck's full lips curved ever so slightly. Was he amused at something the mayor said, or laughing at the mayor himself? She could never be sure with Buck. Her gaze lingered on his proud stance, the long dark hair curling over his collar, the shadow of a beard on his chin.

As if sensing her scrutiny, he glanced at her. One

eyebrow lifted in silent acknowledgment.

Sunny looked away, her palms suddenly sweaty. "Buck doesn't want a haircut, does he?"

"No, he doesn't." The sweetness had drained out of Leanne's voice, replaced by an I-can't-believe-this-is-happening-the-night-before-my-wedding tone. "There are photographs to consider." Leanne released Sunny's hands and walked away.

Sunny turned on her phone and texted herself a reminder: duct tape. It wouldn't be the first time she'd used it on Buck.

~

Bright and early Saturday morning, Buck stood barefoot in his stepfather's kitchen, wishing for the thousandth time in his life that Sunny DeStefano would go away. How could anybody be so cheerful, so optimistic? She reminded him way too much of things he'd never have.

She stood waiting for him just beyond the screen door, hair clippers pointed straight at his heart. "You. Sit."

The morning sun streamed onto the back porch where Sunny had set up a chair for barbering. The scent of lilac rode the breeze, dousing the Virginia mountain town in its annual explosion of sweetness. He closed his eyes and inhaled. He hadn't realized how much he'd missed it. Not much lilac in the swamp.

"I'm waiting." Sunny's sandal-clad foot tapped the floor boards, her silver anklet twinkling in the sunlight. Her short, black skirt revealed a pair of long, tanned legs, muscles taut with impatience.

"Ought to be a crime to ambush a man this early in the morning." Buck pushed his tangled hair out of his eyes and cast a lazy look at his stepfather. "Let me guess. The bride wants me to get a haircut."

Donnie sat reading the newspaper at the other end of the porch, his salt-and-pepper hair trimmed up neat. He nodded without looking over. "Yep."

Silver bangle bracelets clinked together as Sunny crossed her arms over her frilly white top, her glossy dark hair spilling over her shoulders. "Leanne does not want you photobombing the pictures with your swamp dog look. Be a good usher and do what she wants."

Buck ran a calloused hand down his bristled jaw. "Folks expect a Louisiana swamp boat owner to look the part, *chere*."

Donnie chuckled. "Tourists buy that fake Cajun accent?"

Buck grinned. "Yes, if the tips are any indication."

Sunny blew out a breath. "I have a long list of clients today. Are you going to let me cut your hair, or do I have to call the bride?"

A look of panic flashed on Donnie's face. "Better do what she says."

Buck had been back in Lilac less than twenty-four hours, and the tension around Donnie's house was thicker than bayou fog. Of course, Donnie and Leanne had brought it on themselves by inviting the entire town to the celebration.

Buck sighed, shoved his hands into the pockets of his jeans, and sauntered onto the back porch. If he ever got married—*not* that he had any plans of ever getting married— he'd do it up simple like Reo and Jack. Immediate family and a couple friends. Quiet ceremony. Lunch afterwards. Thinking about the three-ring circus he was about to be a part of made him want to hop in his car and disappear. Thank God, tomorrow this time he'd be on the road, heading back to New Orleans. All of this would be a memory.

The old wooden chair creaked as he sat down.

Sunny snapped open a large towel and draped it across his chest. "Hard to believe you let me pretend-shave you with a butter knife when we were kids."

"For a price." He stretched out his legs and slanted a pointed look up at her.

Sunny rolled her eyes. "Are you referring to that sorry kiss you planted on me when I was all of twelve? Please." She motioned Donnie over and handed him her phone. "Okay, Mister Groom, make yourself useful. Take a picture of Buck and me doing the deed. We'll send it to Leanne and make her laugh."

Sunny turned on the clippers and aimed them at Buck's head.

Buck's hand shot out and circled her wrist, the electric clippers buzzing between them. Vibration rattled up his arm as her wide-eyed gaze locked with his. He shook his head. "No clippers."

Flash! "Got it!" Donnie said.

Sunny snatched the clippers from his grasp with a huff.

Donnie showed them the image and laughed. "Looks like you two want to kill each other."

The corner of Buck's mouth curved. "Sounds about right."

Sunny had been a fixture around the Greene home for as long as Buck could remember, his half-sister Reo's best friend since kindergarten. The girls' endless giggling used to drive him outside faster than any recess bell. Seeing Sunny last night in the moonlight, he couldn't deny she'd grown into a beautiful woman. There'd been a time when he'd thought there might be something between them, but that had been a foolish teenager's dream.

"I'm leaving you two alone against my better judgment." Donnie pointed at the back yard. "Promise I won't find one of you tied to that tree when I get back."

Buck snorted. "That was fifteen years ago. Today I'd just lock her in a closet."

Sunny batted her lashes at him. "Not before I cut off your ear."

"Surrender, Buck. She's armed." Donnie chuckled. "Thanks for the haircut."

"My pleasure." Sunny gave Donnie a hug.

Donnie paused as he pulled open the screen door. "Sorry your parents couldn't make it up for the wedding. Give them my best."

"I'll do that."

Buck tilted his head. Sunny's parents had been fixtures around town forever. The perfect Lilac family. "Where'd your parents go?"

Sunny lifted sections of his hair and examined them. "Florida."

"Leaving you in charge of the salon?"

"You got it." She tugged a lock. "When's the last time you cut your hair?"

Buck shrugged. "Who knows? Wouldn't be cutting it now if I'd stayed home."

Sunny dropped the hair she'd been holding. "Don't you want to be in Donnie's wedding?"

"Sure, for Donnie. Just not a big fan of marriage." His own mother had five children by five different men and had married all of them except Buck's father Spike.

He scowled at the sudden flash of sympathy on Sunny's face. As a kid he'd gotten good at dodging Lilac residents who offered pity to his face when they weren't gossiping behind his back. Poor Buck Day. Abandoned by his father and his mother. What a shame.

"This dress looks like a bag of cotton candy." The screen door banged open and Gina stomped out of the kitchen onto the back porch, her puffy pink dress bouncing around her knees like a balloon. "I told you I didn't want to do this. Oh. Hi, Sunny."

Great. Pity and complaining. This day was going to be even more stressful than he'd predicted if things didn't lighten up. Buck took a deep breath. "You look nice."

Sunny stepped forward to give Gina a quick hug. "Aren't you excited about being in the wedding, S.B?"

Buck's brow furrowed. "Who's S.B.?"

"Sleeping Beauty," Sunny replied, her pert little nose in the air. "He wouldn't understand, would he, S.B.?"

"No, he wouldn't." Gina shot Buck an irritated look. "I would be excited if I could've invited Remy."

"Who's Remy?" Sunny asked, her questioning gaze shooting between Gina and Buck.

"We've been over that." Buck regretted his curt reply as soon as the words were out of his mouth. Why was he finding it so hard to be patient? He had to keep reminding himself Gina was only a kid. "Did you talk to your father yet?"

Gina scowled. "No." She turned to Sunny, her expression dreamy. "Remy is one of the tour boat captains. He's really cute. I wanted to invite him to the wedding, but Buck said no."

Buck fought to keep his voice calm. "He's way too old for you."

Gina lifted her chin in the air. "When I'm eighteen there'll be nothing you can do about it." She ran into the house, the screen door banging shut behind her.

Sunny set down her comb. "What's so bad about Remy?"

Buck crossed his arms. "Did Leanne hire you to cut hair or gossip?"

"Hello? Have you forgotten who discovered you even had a second sister?" Sunny planted her hands on her hips.

"That gives you the right to gossip about her?" Buck clamped his jaw tight before he said something he'd regret. He'd never forget how embarrassed he'd felt the day his sister Reo dragged eight-year-old Sunny upstairs to his bedroom and made her repeat the whispered gossip she'd overheard at the Up Do. His mother Carly Day was living twenty miles away in Carsondale. She was married again with a daughter—her fifth child—and hadn't even thought to pick up the phone and tell her other four children.

"So, I care about Gina. Sue me." Sunny went back to combing his hair.

Buck shifted his shoulders, trying to settle into the hard-backed chair. "You don't hear me asking why your parents moved to Florida. Ouch!"

Sunny's comb pulled at a knot. "They retired."

"Always pegged them as Lilac lifers." The comb scraped his scalp and stuck in a tangle. "Hey!" He angled his shoulders sideways, sliding his hair from her grasp. "How about a shampoo?"

"How long will it take you to shower?" Sunny glanced at her cell phone.

Buck rubbed the back of his neck. "Can't you wash it?"

The corner of her mouth curved. "And give you a nice scalp massage, I suppose?"

He arched an eyebrow at her. "Give you a big tip."

Sunny snatched a bottle of shampoo from her supply bag and marched into the kitchen, letting the screen door slam behind her. "Come here."

He followed her into the kitchen. "You're kidding."

She leaned her hip against the sink. "Well, I'm not climbing in the shower with you."

"Why not? We went to the swimming hole together," he said.

"Don't act like it was anything special. Half the kids in town were skinny-dipping that night." Sunny got up on tip-toe and draped the towel across his back, her fingers cool on his neck. "Bend over."

He glanced over his shoulder. "In another context, that comment could be construed as sexual harassment."

Sunny narrowed her gaze. "Do I have to get the duct tape?"

"You're even bossier than you used to be." He lowered his head into the sink, his back muscles cracking with relief as he stretched forward. Closing his eyes as warm water coursed through his hair, he relaxed into the heat, feeling the tension drain out of his neck muscles. He couldn't remember the last time he'd had a scalp massage.

A sudden blast of hot water singed his head. He jerked to the side. "Hey, watch it!"

Sunny stared at him, brown eyes wide with innocence. "Too warm?"

"What are you, ten? Fix the temperature." He blew out a breath as the water cooled down.

Her phone buzzed. Out of the corner of his eye Buck watched Sunny reading a text message. "Mrs. Merriweather wants me to style her sister, too." She poured on the shampoo and lathered it up. "Do you remember her? She used to live in the big blue house on Madison Street. Her husband just retired from some big airline. He was a pilot."

Buck closed his eyes, lost in the tingly feeling of her fingers kneading his scalp. "Could you please stop talking?"

"Most clients like me to talk. You don't have to talk back, Mr. Big Tipper." She squirted his face with the sprayer.

Water dripped down his nose as she rambled on. Donnie should've warned him the price of a haircut was listening to gossip. He wished he could close his ears as easily as he could close his eyes.

"Mrs. Merriweather says she wouldn't know what was going on in town if I didn't come to the Mountain Mist senior community to cut hair. Mr. Deutsch calls me his little ray of sunshine. Remember Dewey's dad? He's in the early stages of Alzheimer's." Her fingertips scrubbed hard as she rinsed out the lather. "Mr. Quisenbury's the only one who doesn't like to talk much."

Buck's body tensed. "Mr. who?"

"Mr. Quisenbury."

Buck jerked upright, whipping his head out of the sink. Water streamed down his face.

Sunny shrieked and jumped back. "You got me all wet!"

He grabbed a dishtowel and dried his face. Water ran in rivulets beneath his tee shirt, all the way to his bare feet. A shiver ran down back. "Mr. Quisenbury. What's his first name?"

Sunny looked at him like he was crazy. "Norton. No, wait. Norbert."

"How old is he?"

"Eighty-something. Why?"

Figure the odds. The senior community. Donnie had said something about the new facility, but Buck had never thought of looking there. He rubbed the towel through his wet hair, his heart pounding. Eighty was way too old. A distant relative of his father's?

Buck strode outside onto the back porch and dropped into the chair. Most folks had only known his father as Spike, a wandering biker who'd swept Carly Day onto the back of his Harley and sped into the sunset. Very few people in this town knew his father's real name.

Norel Quisenbury.

Buck had accepted long ago there'd be no joyous reunion with the man who'd only stayed around long enough to give Buck his DNA and a nickname. Their last short encounter a decade before had been painfully awkward. Yet, the need to know more about the man who'd fathered him ran deep in his bones, leaving a gaping hole in a place that might have held family pride.

"I'll see you at the reception." Sunny's voice drifted through the screen door.

"Wait!" He yanked open the door and hurried into the kitchen.

Sunny sat with her back to him, dark hair draped over one shoulder, her phone pressed to her ear.

Buck cleared his throat. "Um, my hair."

"Just a minute." She angled her head over her shoulder, hand covering her phone. "You need to clean up your mess." Her pointed gaze dropped to the wet floor, her tone all business. "What were you saying, Phil?"

Buck ripped paper towels from the roll and threw them onto the puddles around the sink as Sunny continued her conversation. Sometime during the past few years that irritating schoolgirl giggle had changed into a woman's laugh, warm and inviting. The kind of laugh a man wanted to hear on a cold winter night.

"You're kidding!" she exclaimed. "I can't wait to see it."

Buck wiped up the linoleum and tossed the wet paper towels into the trash, searching his memory for Lilac residents named Phil. He drummed his fingers on the counter, waiting for her to hang up. "Who's Phil? And what's he got that you can't wait to see?"

"Ha-ha." Sunny stood, smoothing her hands over her skirt. "You'll meet him tonight. He's an engineer at the solar energy plant."

"What does he want to show you? His big house or his new car?" Seemed like all the women he met these days had dollar signs in their eyes. Could women in Lilac be any different?

Sunny's gaze narrowed. "As a matter of fact, neither. He's restoring a vintage Mustang and wants me to see the new paint job."

"Right." Buck snorted. "Are you going to cut my hair or not?"

"Not." She glanced at the clock. "Your time's up."

"What about the wedding pictures?" he sputtered.

"Should've thought about that before you started insulting me. I told you I had clients waiting. It's not my problem you refused to listen." She strode out of the kitchen onto the back porch.

Buck gripped the counter. Uh-oh. For all his griping, he really didn't want to ruin the photos. Donnie didn't deserve that. He jogged onto the porch where Sunny was packing up her supplies. "Don't leave."

She threw her bag over her shoulder and walked past him, eyes straight forward. "Shave. Pull your hair into a ponytail. You own a swamp boat. Folks'll understand."

~

Sunny jammed the key into the ignition of her lime green VW Bug, her gaze fixed on the small silver cross clipped to her visor. *Please, God, give me patience.*

Why did Buck bring out the worst in her? They went at each other like cats in a bag. He accused her of gossiping about Gina, implied she liked Phil for his money. What had she done to deserve that? With everyone else, she could keep her thoughts to herself, say the right things, like the Little-Miss-Customer-Service her mother had raised her to be. Being around Buck removed all her filters. Words spilled out of her mouth before she could control them.

Thank goodness, he never came into the salon. There, she had to watch every word she said for fear of offending a client. Her dad had said more than once that being in business meant being a diplomat.

She glanced in the mirror, blinking away the moisture that threatened her mascara. What in the world had made Buck jump and splash water all over her? It was like he'd been struck by lightning. She'd had clients tell her they sometimes got their best ideas when Sunny was massaging their scalps, but Buck's reaction was ridiculous. She pressed a tissue to the damp spots on her blouse. Her clients expected her to be fashionably dressed, with perfectly styled hair and flawless makeup. If she walked into her next appointment at Mountain Mist with wet clothes and raccoon eyes, she'd never hear the end of it. *You are a walking advertisement for the Up Do salon,* her mom always said.

Her mother. She would have a fit about Sunny wasting her time arguing with Buck on the morning of a wedding. There was still the bridal party to style, not to mention attaching Leanne's veil. Sunny's phone rang.

"Where are you?" Jill Vogel, the event coordinator from the Mountain Mist retirement community, asked. "Every five minutes somebody wheels over to the counter and demands to know when you're coming."

Sunny cringed. "Please tell me you're joking."

"Of course, I'm joking." Jill chuckled. "Some of your clients are getting antsy, though. They insisted I call and make sure you're not broken down on the side of the road. You brought this on yourself by always being early."

She glanced over her shoulder at Donnie's front door and nibbled her bottom lip. Leanne would never forgive her if Buck showed up with a sloppy ponytail. "Give me twenty minutes."

"Okay, but hurry. The residents want to get to the church early and catch up on all the gossip."

Sunny climbed out of the car, supply bag gripped tightly in her hand, and marched up Donnie's front walk. She was the manager of the Up Do. She needed to keep her word to Leanne, even if it meant putting up with Buck's obnoxious behavior. Just because he was disagreeable didn't mean she had to be.

She glanced up at the bright blue sky. "You can help me do this," she whispered. Ever since her parents had moved away, Sunny had found herself asking God for help a lot more frequently. *Trust in the Lord*, her father always said. *Everybody else wants something.*

She took a deep breath. She'd been raised in the hair salon business. Slept in a crib in the office while her mother worked. Sat on her father's shoulders while he made bank deposits. Dealing with people was second nature to her.

Help me learn how to deal with Buck.

Sunny pushed the doorbell and waited. Nothing. She

rapped on the door. When Buck didn't respond, she pounded harder. Suddenly the door swung open and she stumbled against his chest. She looked up at him and gasped.

His long dark hair covered one cheek like a scraggly curtain. The hair on the other side of his head was buzzed short.

Her jaw dropped. "What did you do?"

Strong hands gripped her arms and settled her on her feet. "Found Donnie's clippers." His proud grin faded. "What? Does it look bad?"

"You look like an extra in a horror film." Sunny grabbed his hand. "Come on." She pulled him through the house to the back porch and plugged in her clippers. She pointed a finger at him. "Do not say one word."

For the first time in all the years she'd known him, Buck listened. He actually sat still and closed his eyes.

Sunny got to work, all five senses focused on the crisis before her. Trimming here, sculpting there, she switched clipper guards with rapid movements, creating the style she envisioned in her mind. Her fingers only paused once over a jagged scar on the side of his neck. Where had that come from? He hadn't had that as a kid. Finally, she turned off the clippers and handed him a mirror.

"Ta-da! From zombie to usher in ten minutes." She studied him and nodded. The short cut emphasized his strong jaw and bright blue eyes. He'd look handsome in the pictures. "Don't be surprised if people think you joined the Marines."

He took the mirror she handed him and ran a hand over his buzzed hair. "Won't do much for the swamp boat clientele."

"Pierce your ear and wear a bandana." She turned away

and shoved her supplies into her bag.

"What made you come back?" he asked.

His voice was so low, she almost didn't hear him. What would he say if she told him the truth? "I prayed for patience."

His brow furrowed. "You what?"

Ouch. He didn't physically lean away from her, but it sure felt like he did. She stepped back. "I needed to keep my word. I have a business to run." She snatched up her bag. "Now, if you'll excuse me, there's a room full of senior citizens who'll shoot me on sight if I don't get over to Mountain Mist."

Buck jumped to his feet. "You're going there now?"

"Yes." What was she thinking, mentioning prayer to Buck? She pulled open the screen door and scurried from the back porch into the kitchen.

"Give me a minute. I'm coming with you." He followed her inside the house.

Yeah, right. Sunny scurried across the living room to the front door. If she hurried she could finish her Mountain Mist clients before lunch.

"Sunny!" Buck shouted. He snatched the tote bag from her grasp.

She spun around.

With his buzzed hair and intense expression, he glared at her like a soldier on a mission. "Please," he said, lowering his voice. "Start the car. I'll change while you drive."

She yanked her bag away from him. "Why should I?"

Buck shoved his hands in his pockets, a self-conscious expression on his face. "Your comment about praying for patience. I'd just been thinking I needed patience with Gina, and then you said that. Weird."

The anger drained from her. She opened her mouth to speak, to tell him coincidences like that weren't coincidences at all, but the words didn't come.

"I need to go with you to Mountain Mist." Buck said, his voice solemn. "I think your Mr. Quisenbury might be related to Spike."